W9-CRM-446

AMISH INN MYSTERIES™

Secrets *of the* Amish Diary

Rachael Phillips

Annie's®
AnniesFiction.com

Library of Congress-in-Publication Data
Secrets of the Amish Diary / by Rachael Phillips
p. cm.
I. Title
2015916665

AnniesFiction.com
(800) 282-6643
Amish Inn Mysteries™
Series Creator: Shari Lohner
Series Editor: Shari Lohner
Cover Illustrator: Kelley McMorris

10 11 12 13 14 | Printed in China | 9 8 7 6 5 4 3 2 1

A new life as an innkeeper . . . what was I thinking?

Gripping the sink plunger, Liz Eckardt considered inviting the real estate agent who had emphasized the Olde Mansion Inn's state-of-the-art kitchen to share her morning. She shoved the plunger down-up-down-up-down until the drain finally gave an approving *urp* and water ran freely. Liz scrubbed the sink until it gleamed like the surrounding granite counters and new stainless steel appliances.

With a sigh of relief, she shed her rubber gloves and zapped a mug of tea in the microwave, too annoyed to wait for the copper teakettle to boil. Then she carried her tea to the living room and dropped into the cushy chintz chair behind the walnut desk.

At least she'd avoided the expense of a plumber. After a few sips, the tension in Liz's shoulders relaxed. She loved this room. The elegant yet comfortable furniture that had come with the inn surrounded the marble fireplace, inviting conversation or evenings cozied with good books. Early May sunlight glimmered through tall windows, each topped with stained glass lilies. They overlooked the landscaped grounds where pink-and-white dogwood blossoms rippled in the light breeze.

Despite the few glitches she'd encountered since purchasing the grand Victorian mansion, it already felt like home. As did the quaint town of Pleasant Creek, Indiana, its quiet streets lined with old-fashioned gas lamps and hanging flower baskets. It was so different from her former life in Boston—especially the periodic *clop-clop* of Amish buggy horses passing by outside the inn.

Ahhh . . . She sipped more tea. Owning the Olde Mansion Inn was a dream come true. The first time Liz had visited, her blood pressure dropped five points.

She would help her guests unwind too—once she officially opened for business.

Successfully running an inn would take more effort than sitting in a parlor and drinking tea, of course. And certainly it would take even more than plunging a sink. But she'd conquered other challenges, hadn't she? Liz had attended college and law school on a shoestring budget and graduated from both near the top of her class. Then she'd built a high-powered career as a patent attorney at a prestigious law firm, all while raising her godson, Steve, whose parents had died in a car accident.

It was a solid résumé of meeting life's challenges.

But could she cook breakfast for five to ten people without incinerating the bacon or carbonizing the coffee cake? Could she keep five bathrooms spotless?

Thank goodness she'd found Sarah Yoder, her part-time employee. None of Liz's Boston cleaning women could match the eighteen-year-old Amish girl's efficiency and energy. Together, they would keep the Olde Mansion Inn running smoothly until Liz could afford more help.

In the meantime, Liz would grab what free moments she could to pursue the mystery that had brought her to Pleasant Creek—the *real* reason she'd come.

She'd come to discover the truth about her late mother's past.

Gazing at her mom's childhood picture displayed on the fireplace mantel, she nestled into the soft baby quilt that lay across the back of her chair. The quilt, with its intricate star design, had also belonged to her mother, Abigail Byler Eckardt. Liz reached into a desk drawer and pulled out the diary she had received at the reading of her mother's will. Its faded pages told the heartrending story of how Abigail had left her Pleasant Creek Amish family decades before, a story Liz had never heard while her mother lived.

Why, Mom? Why did you keep such an important part of your past a secret? So far, Liz had read nothing that would explain her mother's motivation.

Abigail also avoided using names, although she mentioned a host of loved ones—besides her *Vater* and *Mutter,* sisters and brothers, she spoke of grandparents, aunts, uncles, and cousins. She'd left them all behind one autumn night, slipping out of her parents' farmhouse to walk to a neighboring town's bus station and travel to Boston—a city she'd never seen.

I knew I was leaving forever, her mother wrote. *My steps were watered with tears.*

Liz, her own eyes blurring, ran her fingers over the tattered yellow cover of the diary. "I don't know why you didn't tell me about your background, Mom. But you gave me the diary. You must have wanted me to find the answers—to find my family here."

Family. The word echoed through the empty chambers of her heart. She barely remembered her father, as he had died when she was just a preschooler. Now her mother was gone too, and her godson, Steve, whom she had raised, was stationed far away in Kosovo—

The front door chimes, insistent as church bells, interrupted Liz's thoughts. She glanced out a window, surprised to see two older women standing on her doorstep.

The taller of the two wore an enormous red straw hat with orange and purple flowers sticking out at odd angles. The shorter one wore her shining gray hair styled in a shoulder-length bob. Both carried boxes overflowing with bolts of fabric.

Liz squinted. *Pleasant Creek's version of a welcoming committee?* When she opened the front door, the smiles that met her seemed to [illegible]an the inn's entrance.

"You must be Liz!" Despite her load, the hatless woman extended [illegible] manicured hand. "I'm Mary Ann Berne."

[illegible]" Liz grasped the proffered hand, wondering how the [illegible]r name.

[illegible]die Schwarzentruber," the taller woman said. The [illegible]er hat bobbed with each word. Below the hat twinkly blue eyes framed by laugh wrinkles peered back at Liz. "I'm your friendly crazy quilter, and there isn't a better one on earth. But we'll talk about that later."

"Yes, these are heavy." Mary Ann shifted her box. "Excuse us. Our backs aren't what they used to be."

Despite her confusion, Liz reached out to take the box, but the woman strode past her and entered the foyer and rotunda. She headed straight for the two semi-empty rooms on the first floor whose functions Liz had pondered since she'd purchased the place. Sadie followed suit, and they set their boxes on the hardwood floor.

Sadie looked around the room with satisfaction and clasped her hands. "I can hardly wait to get going again! You don't think our customers have forgotten us, do you?"

Liz blinked. *Their customers?*

"Not likely," Mary Ann said. "I think we're going to have our best year yet. You'll see." She gave Liz's shoulder an exultant pat and hurried out the front door, Sadie on her heels.

What on earth? Liz remained rooted in place and watched wide-eyed as the women opened their patchwork-patterned van and hauled more fabric up the walkway toward the inn's front porch.

Say something, Lawyer Liz, she commanded herself. *Do something!*

2

Liz raced outside. "Hold on just a second," she said to Mary Ann and Sadie as they approached the front steps carrying more boxes of fabric, "I don't know what customers you were referring to, but I own this bed-and-breakfast now—"

"Of course you do." Mary Ann beamed. "And we couldn't be happier. Now things can finally get back to normal." She balanced her box on the cream-color railing, slipped behind Liz, and edged the front door open again. Sadie followed Mary Ann to their rooms with Liz trailing like an afterthought.

Not *their* rooms. Liz shook herself. Her rooms. In her inn. The inn that had swallowed every penny she possessed.

"The sign usually goes here." Sadie gestured to an area outside the rooms. "But if you'd prefer it go somewhere else, we could talk about other options once we're settled in."

Liz blinked. "No. No sign anywhere. Now I'm afraid I'm going to have to ask you both to lea—"

"Don't worry, dearie. It's very tasteful." Sadie straightened her wild hat.

Liz slapped her tightening forehead as the woman strode outside, flowers flapping, presumably to get another load. *This is insane.* As a patent lawyer, Liz had dealt with everything from loony inventors to hostile bureaucracies. Why couldn't she just kick these two women out already?

The doorbell chime drew her to the front door again. She arrived in time to see a UPS truck roaring away, having left two new boxes on her porch. She eyed one of the labels. *Attention: Mary Ann Berne*, it read, listing the Olde Mansion Inn's address.

How long has that woman been planning this . . . this invasion?

Mary Ann poked her head out the door. "Did the new fabrics come already? Wonderful! I'll help you bring them in." She scooped up one box and carried it inside.

Speechless, Liz glared at the other box. She left it on the step and stormed back into the inn.

"Do you have a headache?" Mary Ann asked her. "Moving can be very stressful. But I know just what you need." Like a conjurer, the woman reached into a large bag and produced the biggest, flakiest-looking, lattice-topped apple pie Liz had ever seen. "Find someplace for this and put on the coffee, will you, dear? We'll dig in after we unload a few more boxes. Setting up a fabric shop is an exhausting endeavor."

"About that," Liz began, "It appears there's been a misunderstanding. This inn was sold to me. Only me. Unless you have some kind of legal paperwork—"

"Oh, there's no paperwork, dear. That's not how we do things around here." Mary Ann smiled warmly. "Our fabric shop has been located in the Olde Mansion Inn for decades. It's tradition. But don't fret. The shop brings in lots of customers, many of whom have family and friends who stay at the inn when they come to town. And we pay monthly rent for the space, of course." With that, Mary Ann went about her business, leaving Liz to stare after her, pie in hand.

A very delicious-smelling pie . . .

No. I will not be swayed by pie. I will call the police. Trying to reason with these two kooky women clearly won't work.

But as Liz carried the pie to the kitchen, it wafted a cinnamony fragrance, as sweet and overwhelming as its baker, and she felt her resolve weaken.

"Oh, no, you don't," Liz muttered to the empty room. She set the pie on the center island. "If those freeloading grandmas think plying me with pie will allow them take over my inn, they've got another thing coming."

She pulled her cell phone from her pocket, started to punch in numbers, and then stopped. Should she alienate two citizens of this small town before her business even opened? Two cheerful and—dare she say—likable women, despite the fact that they were trespassing? *Perhaps I should try one last time to sort this out myself. I can always call the police later if need be.* Liz took a deep breath and applied herself to grinding beans and brewing. With their mouths full, surely Sadie and Mary Ann would stay quiet long enough that Liz could get in a sane word in edgewise.

But the plan backfired. The pie worked its magic on Liz instead. After one mouthwatering bite, she, like a ten-year-old, gobbled up the entire giant wedge Mary Ann had placed on her plate. Instead of asserting her legal rights, Liz could only eke out a reverent, pie-stuffed, "Incredible. Thank you."

"You're so welcome." Mary Ann grinned.

"So-o-o welcome," Sadie echoed, elbowing her partner in crime. Both laughed.

Liz's headache mushroomed. What was so blasted funny?

"It's our shop's name, you know. Sew Welcome. S-e-w." Mary Ann slid another wedge of pie onto Liz's plate. "Being new to the area, you have a lot to process. But you'll catch onto everything after you've lived here awhile." She glanced at her watch. "Coffee break's over for us."

Sadie stood. "Lots more boxes to bring in."

Liz watched them go, wondering when letter-of-the-law attorney Liz Eckardt had turned into such a pushover. But they *had* mentioned something about rent, hadn't they?

Her only employee poked her nose around the corner, and Liz quickly wiped crumbs off her face.

"Miss Eckardt, I finished painting the third-floor bathroom."

"Thanks, Sarah. Next, you can scrape any paint off the floor or window, and then clean the bathroom thoroughly. But first, have a snack." Liz pushed the pie across the shining mahogany table. "Mary Ann Berne brought it."

"Mrs. Berne? It looks scrumptious. I should have guessed." The girl tucked away a tendril of blond hair that had escaped her white *Kapp,* sat, and helped herself.

"So Mary Ann's pies are famous around here?" Liz asked. Perhaps Sarah, now under the influence of baked goods, could provide her with a little insider information.

Sarah paused midbite. "As famous as her mother's and grandmother's. It's a family tradition. Almost every year Mrs. Berne's pies win first prize at the county fair."

"I imagine so. She's a champion seamstress too, I suppose?"

"She and Mrs. Schwarzentruber have run a sewing and quilting shop ever since I can remember. They're moving in, aren't they?"

"That's clearly their intention." Liz frowned. "You don't seem surprised."

Sarah chuckled. "They're good friends with my mother. With everyone, actually. They've been eager to set up their store again ever since the former owner moved out and put it up for sale. Sew Welcome has been a part of this inn for a long time." Some of Sarah's usual reserve returned, and she rose, brushing crumbs from her apron. "I'd better get back to work. You'll want everything perfect when your first guests arrive." She bustled away, leaving Liz feeling like a teenager goofing off.

Taking another bite of pie, she pondered the notion of a fabric shop in the inn, struggling to find reasons to reject the whole concept. It certainly wasn't something she would have thought of on her own. But the truth was . . . she kind of liked the idea. She loved to quilt—if only she'd had more time for it in recent years. And she couldn't deny that the additional foot traffic would benefit her business.

With a sigh, she stood, muttering, "I'd better see what those two women are up to now." Why, she didn't know. Thus far, her protests hadn't registered on their radar.

Sure enough, the sign Sadie had spoke of hung outside "their" rooms on a rotunda wall. It *was* tasteful, Liz had to admit. It showed an intricate miniature quilt with appliquéd letters: Sew Welcome Shop.

Liz noted that the original two "intruders" had now multiplied to five, all of whom were bringing in boxes.

"Here she is!" Sadie grasped Liz's hand, twirled her in an impromptu dance, and then gestured at their audience. "Come meet the rest of the Material Girls."

Liz surveyed the small group. *Material Girls?* None of them resembled 1980s pop star Madonna who'd made the song famous.

"Our quilting group," Mary Ann said, no doubt reading the blank look on Liz's face. "Silk, satin, calico, burlap, bamboo—we Material Girls sew all kinds of material."

Sadie grabbed a fabric rose from a box of notions. With the rose clasped between her teeth, she slunk around the room, humming a loud off-key rendition of *Don't Cry for Me, Argentina.*

Oblivious to Sadie's surprisingly sinuous performance, Mary Ann introduced Liz to the three newcomers: Opal Ringenberg, Caitlyn Ross, and Naomi Mason. Dark-haired Naomi looked fortyish, about Liz's age, and flashed an infectious grin. Naomi owned the bakery, Sweet Everything, that was located next door to the inn. Opal, with graying dark hair and a gentle voice, wore a print dress with a lace collar. Twenty-something Caitlyn, who sported short, red-streaked hair and a small butterfly tattoo on her neck, said hello. Then she partnered with Sadie in the tango, singing the *Argentina* lyrics in a mellow tone.

"These girls are marvelous, and we work very well together. But we lack a key person . . ." Mary Ann fixed Liz with a perfect salesman's gaze. "You."

How did Mary Ann know she quilted? Liz sputtered, "I-I'm not an expert seamstress."

"I'm not either." Naomi joined the persuasion campaign. "But I've learned from the others."

The "please" in Naomi's voice almost drew a "yes" from Liz on the spot. Something told her that she and Naomi could click. But, still, these women were basically strangers . . .

The doorbell's chime saved Liz from replying. She opened the door to find a middle-aged Amish woman and two young girls staring at her. She caught her breath at the sight of them. One girl, who appeared to be about twelve, looked exactly like Liz's mother had as a teen—a living replica of the fireplace mantel photo. Liz didn't mean to be rude and stare, but she couldn't pull her gaze away from the girl.

"May I help you?" Liz finally managed, the words sticking in her throat.

"You made it!" Mary Ann hurried to the front door. She introduced the family to Liz. "This is Miriam Borkholder, one of the best quilters around, and her daughters, Grace and Keturah."

Liz grasped Miriam's work-roughened hand, smiled into the woman's serene indigo eyes, and gulped. Beyond the warm smile that answered her own, she sensed a connection that two people from different worlds should not be capable of feeling.

"Hello, Miss Eckardt." Little-girl voices blended into one. Keturah, who informed Liz she was six, flitted about like an aproned fairy with braided pigtails. But it was Grace and her likeness to Liz's late mother who took Liz's breath away. *Could it possibly be . . . ?*

"H-hello." Liz wasn't usually prone to stuttering, but today, her mouth felt like stretched-out elastic.

"I was pleased to hear Sew Welcome would open again," Miriam said. "Thank you for making that possible."

As if Liz had had any say about it. "Uh, well . . ."

"Mary Ann and Sadie are lovely women," Miriam continued. "They really know their craft. Do you quilt too?"

"A little. My mother taught me when I was young, but I haven't had much time for it lately." At the tender memory, Liz's throat tightened. *Breathe,* she commanded herself. *Talk.* "However, Mom leaned toward more contemporary patterns."

They chatted about quilting for a few minutes, and then Miriam and her girls left. Liz exhaled as she watched them go. She longed to know them better but feared she would scare them off by hugging them like long-lost relatives. Ridiculous, since she possessed absolutely no evidence of their blood link other than a gut feeling and Grace's resemblance to Liz's mother. Many Amish with German or Swiss heritage had fair coloring. She couldn't go around hugging every blond, blue-eyed person who wore a bonnet or beard.

Yet Liz couldn't ignore Grace either. That child, with her thick braids, fathomless blue-gray eyes, and slightly sideways, full-lipped smile, looked like her mother's young clone when compared to the photograph. Of course the childhood picture of Liz's mother was that of a teenager—presumably taken soon after Abigail had left her family, since having one's picture taken wasn't allowed in the Amish community—and she was dressed like a typical teen. But the striking resemblance was impossible to miss.

While the Material Girls chattered and unpacked, Liz wandered into the foyer and dropped onto a settee. Why did she suddenly feel so drained? The stately old grandfather clock had chimed only half past ten. Maybe it was because she was crashing after consuming more sugar in thirty minutes than she'd eaten in the past six months. Or perhaps it was because she might have just met long-lost relatives that she'd only recently learned even existed. The alien quilters who had taken over part of her inn probably had a little to do with her current state too.

The bang of a hammer vibrated through her temples.

A carpenter was building more shelves in Liz's side parlors. Correction—in the Sew Welcome Shop.

When had that guy arrived? During her stumbling conversation with Miriam? Liz had no doubt as to how he'd entered the house. Caitlyn zipped past Liz and opened the door for yet another friend. This one sported green hair.

Mary Ann bustled into the foyer. "Sorry about the noise. But you don't have guests yet, right?"

"Not yet. But soon—"

"The girls and I will have us settled into the shop in no time. I can't tell you how happy I am to see the inn opening again. Our big families love to visit Pleasant Creek, you know." Mary Ann reached into her exquisitely quilted bag. "Goodness, in all the excitement, I forgot to take care of business." She thrust an envelope at Liz. "Here's our deposit, plus the first month's rent. We pay on the first day of every month. Calvin!" she yelled over her shoulder. "We need more shelves on the south wall." Mary Ann strode briskly back to the group and continued to issue congenial orders, which everyone scrambled to carry out.

Liz opened the envelope.

Whoa. The size of the check resuscitated her. At the thought of this regular income, possibilities paraded through Liz's mind: It would swell her pitiful rainy-day fund, and she could enhance the gazebo with additional landscaping. Perhaps she could even take the vacation she'd postponed indefinitely when she bought the Olde Mansion Inn.

Am I nuts? Liz gripped her head in her hands. *Do I really want these presumptuous people in my inn, in my life, every day?*

Yes.

Yes, she did.

The discovery rattled her almost as much as the check. Her attorney side pointed a stern finger: *Sign nothing,* nothing, *until background checks, credit ratings, zoning permits, etc., etc., are reviewed.* Yes, Lawyer Liz would do all that.

But the colorful group of women in the other room had extended eager hands across the empty space in her heart. Back in Boston, her intimate friendships had taken years to establish. She'd never been truly close to Matt, her ex-boyfriend, despite their extended history. Yet within a few hours, these wacky but wonderful Indiana quilters had made her feel like a valued part of their group. They had made her feel at home.

She lectured Lawyer Liz. *Not only will these women provide rental income, they'll bring in other business. Sarah's right. They know everyone in Pleasant Creek. Mary Ann's family has lived here for generations. Plus she may be of help in my search for Mom's family.*

Right now, the only clues about the mysterious family that Liz possessed were her mother's diary and star quilt with the initials E.H. The Material Girls could prove to be the key to finding her relatives.

Wasn't that the main reason she'd come to Indiana?

Besides, if she evicted Mary Ann and Sadie, the locals would ride Liz, tarred and feathered, out of Pleasant Creek on a rail . . . or on a quilting frame, whatever the local custom dictated.

That would not be good for business or family research. Or for Liz.

She stuck the check in her desk and then returned to the Sew Welcome Shop, only to encounter Mary Ann again, armed with a picnic basket. The energetic woman and other similarly equipped Material Girls, followed by Calvin the carpenter and other helpers, all spilled out into the foyer. Only Sadie was missing.

"I think we have a deal," Liz said. "I'll draw up some paperwork."

"If you must." Mary Ann nodded and laughed, a silvery, shiny sound that matched her hair. "In the meantime, we brought lunch." She turned to Calvin. "Of course, you're invited to join us."

He smiled. "Thanks."

"Oh my, I really packed my basket to the top." Mary Ann's smile drooped ever so slightly as her basket inched downward. Calvin quickly grabbed it. "Thank you, dear. I just don't have the oomph I used to."

Liz tried to visualize Mary Ann with more oomph than she currently possessed. Then her thoughts turned to hostess concerns. She'd like to shoo them into the four-season room, but this gang would not fit at its table.

She called after the procession of hungry helpers, "We can use the dining room—"

Her permission, Liz realized, was strictly moot. They'd already swarmed through its door.

Liz sank back onto the settee. She officially held ownership of this inn, but did her signature mean much in Pleasant Creek?

The doorbell chimed yet again, and Liz answered it for what seemed like the hundredth time that morning.

"Sorry, dear," Sadie said, standing on the top step, "but this guy is an armful."

In her arms, she held an enormous bulldog. He remained unmoving, his eyes closed. Was he even breathing? Drool dripped from his wide mouth. Liz took a step back. Then another.

"Don't worry, Beans is gentle as a lamb." With a mighty heave, Sadie plunged through the door and deposited the dog on a nearby rug.

Liz's favorite rug.

For the first time, the catatonic canine's stumpy tail moved.

An inch.

"Look at that. He's so glad to be back!" Sadie scratched the dog's ears. "Beans comes with the inn, of course. The poor guy has been pining for his usual spot here since those nasty real estate agents made us move him out. He's been so upset he's hardly eaten a thing."

Liz did not claim to be a dog expert—she'd mostly lived in apartments where pets were forbidden—but apart from his lack of motion, this one looked perfectly plump and healthy. Sadie petted Beans a few more minutes, and his tail wagged once. Twice.

"I'll feed him and take him out during the day," Sadie said. "If you do it before bedtime and in the morning—around six or so—he'll be just fine." She beamed at Liz.

Six o'clock. Every day. *Seriously?* "I don't think I can—"

"Sounds like they're having a real party in there." The older woman motioned toward the dining room. "Let's go!"

"In a minute. I have to . . . take care of something." Liz waited till her new tenant was out of sight, then plopped down on the settee again.

She needed to take care of something, all right. Herself.

Liz needed space. And oxygen.

Beans's right eye s-l-o-w-l-y inched open. He stared at Liz, unblinking, and then let out a low *woof.*

Liz closed her eyes.

Beans was the least of her problems.

What kind of small-town craziness have I gotten myself into?

3

Taking the Boston subway is like paying good money to ride a runaway horse. I never seem to make the right connections.

Reading her mother's diary and sipping morning tea in the four-season room, Liz chuckled. Strange how she could experience a similar sensation in Pleasant Creek. Mary Ann wasn't the only horse that had galloped her along unplanned routes!

Many friendly townsfolk had offered food and advice to help her adjust, and she'd gratefully accepted it all. But would those connections help her find her family? Liz clicked her mother's childhood photo onto her mind's screen. She'd inherited her mom's fair coloring but otherwise looked like her late father. Miriam's daughter, on the other hand, resembled her mom as if they were long-lost sisters. Liz clicked Grace's face on her mental screen. And then her mom's again.

Grace.

Mom—

I'm going to make myself crazy. Liz closed the diary. Her to-do list could stretch from here to Jaynes Lake, situated behind the inn. Recent rains had coaxed shy spring buds into showing off their brilliant best, but weeds threatened the inn's flower beds. In Boston, Liz had cultivated a few pots of geraniums. However, she'd never waged a major anti-weed campaign. She smeared on sunblock like war paint, donned hat and gloves, and summoned the Internet on her phone. Were those innocent-looking flowered plants weeds or not?

After five minutes in the yard, she considered waving a white flag.

"I'd like to work here."

Liz looked over her shoulder to see a young girl with hopeful eyes. Had God sent a gardening angel? Gratis?

No. She'd have to pay this person. Liz sighed. Even with the Sew Welcome check, she'd rather delay another hire. Yet the teen's direct green eyes held her.

"My name is Kiera Williams. I'm sixteen."

Peeling off muddy gloves, Liz stood and shook her head. "I'm sorry. Perhaps later in the summer."

Kiera eyed the yard, shifting her sparse weight from one worn sandal to the other. She turned back to Liz. "You need help now."

Liz wiped dripping sweat with a nonchalant hand and smiled, but she doubted this sharp-eyed kid bought her act. Multiple flower beds and burgeoning bushes stretched before them in a yard as expansive as a city park but not nearly as manicured. She said lamely, "This is very hard work."

"I live out in the country. I'm used to it." Kiera cracked a knuckle. "I really want to work here."

The girl's wiry arms protruded from a faded pink T-shirt that topped a clean but tattered denim skirt. Kiera's arms reminded Liz of Sadie's—skinny but strong. Especially considering that Sadie had hauled lazy Beans around as if he weighed no more than a stuffed animal. *Do the women in these parts lift cows for exercise?*

She shouldn't let curiosity prolong this unsolicited interview, but she did. "Why do you want a job here?"

Kiera flushed. "I've always loved the Olde Mansion Inn. It looks like a castle."

So this girl had fallen under the spell of the inn's storybook turrets and gables too. Liz tried to harden her resolve, now melting like ice cream in the warm May sun. She couldn't pay another employee.

Her rebellious back reminded Liz she couldn't afford to lie flat for a week every time the weeds grew either. And with indoor and outdoor chores, plus cooking and hosting, she might have to shift her family research to the back burner indefinitely.

"This month, I can offer you five hours of yard work weekly at minimum wage," Liz heard herself say. "Then we'll see."

A quicksilver smile rewarded her. Kiera gestured toward her faded tote. "I brought old clothes. I'll help you now."

Kiera didn't lack initiative. But how could her work clothes look any worse than her interview outfit? Liz pulled her thoughts back to matters at hand. "After you change, you can weed tulip beds and help plant petunias." The nursery guy had said no one could kill petunias. She hoped he was right.

Kiera didn't have to consult a phone. She attacked weeds with a vengeance. Liz revved up hedge trimmers as if she knew what she was doing. If her Amish mother could navigate the subway, Liz could conquer this yard.

No one could miss Pleasant Creek's clock tower in the town square, nor its melodious chimes. Busy since she'd moved, Liz now slowly circled the square in order to admire the details. The arched doorways in the massive limestone tower supported four enormous clock faces and a churchlike steeple. Nearby beds of multicolored tulips formed intricate patchwork patterns. Boxes of freshly planted flowers adorned most businesses' windows. Buildings with Swiss-style balconies and lacy trim made her feel as if she'd crossed an ocean.

Liz parked the gaudy Sew Welcome van she'd borrowed from Mary Ann near the building that housed Cross Furniture Company. A shiny horse hitched to a buggy stood patiently as its bearded Amish owner tied it to one of several hitching posts in a parking lot.

What ambiance. Liz opened the van's back door.

"Need help unloading that rocker?"

The deep voice belonged to a tall man with wide shoulders and dark brown hair. He wore jeans and a wrinkleless navy T-shirt.

"No, thanks." Liz tugged the heavy antique from the van.

"May I carry it someplace for you?"

"Thanks, but Cross Furniture is only one store away—"

"I'm Jackson Cross." A tan, muscular arm slipped between Liz and her burden. He lifted the rocker as if it were made of balsa. "Need repair on the legs?"

"Yes, please." Liz brushed away gnatlike irritation at his persistence. Friendly hazel eyes met hers, and his square jaw softened into a charming grin.

She held the door open as he carried it into the shop filled with superb furniture. There was so much to look at, and Liz couldn't decide which item she loved the most: the oak china cabinet, the cherry dining set, or the huge sleigh bed whose smooth finish begged fingers to run along its carved edges. "You made these?"

"A couple of the pieces. My Amish employees made the rest." He patted her rocker. "No one will ever know your chair was broken."

As Liz signed paperwork, Jackson said, "I understand you're from Boston. How's small-town life treating you so far?"

The Pleasant Creek grapevine strikes again. "It's different, but wonderful. Everyone has been incredibly helpful. I think visitors must fall in love with downtown at first sight."

"The chamber of commerce will appreciate hearing that." Jackson carried the rocker behind the counter. "Once you're settled, please join us. You could advertise your business on the chamber's website, and we certainly would welcome your contributions."

Good idea. But Liz didn't want to commit to joining immediately. She joked, "Judging by how nice the downtown looks, I'm not sure the mayor really needs my contributions."

"The fees don't really go to the mayor, but I know he appreciates your sentiments." Jackson's grin widened. "I'm the mayor."

Liz quickly stammered her way out of the shop but knew she'd made a friend.

And that's all I intend to make. The spark of interest in Jackson's eyes was nice, but after breaking up with Matt, Liz had no plans to rush into another relationship.

Other priorities ruled. Pulling her tablet computer from her purse, she resolutely entered the ornate 1896 courthouse and found the county clerk's office. She could hardly wait to dive into the records.

At Liz's request, the clerk handed her a stack of big black binders filled with birth records.

Paper files only? These dusty old books would slow her progress to buggy's pace. Nevertheless, Liz sat at a clunky table, poring over faded pages covered with inky handwriting.

She found no listing for Abigail Byler. She searched the September 17, 1953, list again. The diary said Liz's mother had been born at home. Perhaps earlier in their history, Amish parents, wary of governmental agencies, had not reported births. But as late as 1953?

Liz searched births a few days before and after her mother's birthday.

No Byler. No Abigail, even. It was a dead end.

A quiver unsettled her stomach. What if she'd given up her law career, her friends, and her future in Boston for a phantom family that haunted a distant corner of nowhereville, where the horses still did their business in the streets?

Shake it off, Liz. Mom had given her the diary for a purpose. Abigail Eckardt did nothing without good reasons.

But why had she kept her background a secret until after her death?

That question ached in Liz's very bones. She would never do something like that to Steve. Her godson knew her life's details, probably better than most biological sons—probably more than he cared to know. They emailed and Skyped whenever they could.

Then again, she'd been extremely close to her mother too . . . Liz bit her lip.

Her fingers drumming on the table resolved in a thump. Surely the "whys" would come to light as she tracked down the facts. Liz pondered the E.H. initials on her mother's baby quilt. Assuming it was approximately Mom's age, Liz delved into 1953 birth and property records, listing families whose names began with *H* and their addresses.

The Hochstedlers alone filled two pages. How would she narrow down the possibilities without interviewing families? And any attempts to do that would destroy Liz's privacy and probably reinforce clan silences. No, her search should remain a secret until she'd uncovered at least a few solid leads. She took photos and typed in some of the information. Years of legal research had taught her "irrelevant" tidbits sometimes proved important.

With the slide show of her mom's childhood photo and Miriam's daughter clicking again in her head, Liz's final sleuthing efforts determined Miriam Borkholder's maiden name: Fischer. Liz briefly scanned her new friend's family records but found no links connecting Miriam and her mother.

Why did I expect to find any?

So far, nothing in the county records confirmed that Abigail Byler Eckardt had ever even set foot in Pleasant Creek.

4

A four-star day! The cordial murmurs of Liz's very first guests floated from the inn's living room as she worked in the kitchen. Four quilters from Louisville, Kentucky, including twin sisters, Violet and Vera, chatted with Emily Hart, a librarian from Ohio. They drooled over the room's fireplace, crystal chandelier and sconces, stained glass, and carved, cushy Victorian sofas. Mary Ann dropped in before she headed home, wielding her usual friendly magic.

Liz carried in another plate of oatmeal-macadamia nut cookies, pausing to admire the quilt block Jill was embroidering. "Beautiful work!"

"It's for my granddaughter's wedding gift," Helen, the oldest quilter, drawled. She pointed to the bonneted infant she was stitching. "This baby resembles her favorite childhood doll, and the cloth comes from the dress she wore on her first day of kindergarten."

Compliments abounded. Liz raised the camera hanging around her neck. "Would you hold that lovely quilt block in front of you, please? I'd like a picture for the inn's album."

The quilting group, after a bout of hair smoothing, posed together.

"You too, Emily." Liz motioned to the librarian, who stood to the side.

"Goodness, no." Emily laughed, but she shook her head vehemently. "Cameras have it in for me."

Liz started to protest, but the doorbell chimed. Her last guest? She quickly snapped a picture of the quilting group, resolving to persuade Emily later.

The bell rang twice more before Liz could open the door.

A graying, stringy-haired man in his mid-fifties frowned at her from the porch. Liz summoned her best smile. "Mr. Clarence Peabody?"

He nodded and lugged in his duffel bag with a huff, his frown deepening.

Liz got him registered and then started to introduce him to the other guests. "Let me introduce you to—"

"My grandfather built this house." Mr. Peabody cast a stern glance around the foyer. "I hope you haven't messed with the structure."

Liz was taken aback by his acerbic tone. How was she supposed to reply to that?

Clarence paced the foyer as if he owned the Olde Mansion. "Can't those women keep it down in there?" he growled in a voice easily overheard in the suddenly quiet living room. "This isn't a party. It's a business, right?"

He informed Liz he would not tolerate TVs or music playing after nine. No showers running either. He didn't like fancy casseroles for breakfast. Just two eggs over easy, four strips of bacon not too well done, and white toast. Plain coffee—no flavored stuff. He hoped she didn't make it so weak he could read a newspaper through it.

Speechless, Liz watched the man ascend to the third-floor Sunset Room.

She'd expected occasional grouches would visit, but she had assumed the grumblers could be tamed by good service, comfortable rooms, and a hefty dose of Mary Ann's pies.

Would this grumpy guest, one of her first, prove her wrong?

"Mr. Peabody, do you know why the Amish don't water-ski?" This first breakfast, Sadie had appointed herself as the inn's social director and sit-down comedienne.

The man transferred his silent scowl from his plate to Sadie. Liz, hurrying back from the kitchen, silently gave thanks that she'd already sent Sarah upstairs to clean.

"Because the horses would drown!" Sadie, Crazy Quilter Extraordinaire, exploded in a minute-long belly laugh.

Earlier, the other guests had chuckled at Sadie's outrageousness. But Peabody's presence, heavy as a soggy quilt, banished all smiles. The Louisville group raised eyebrows and busied themselves with their food. Emily cast a sympathetic look toward Liz.

"You women don't have enough to do, or you wouldn't waste time clucking like a bunch of hens," Mr. Peabody sputtered. "Telling stupid Amish jokes! If you knew the Amish the way I do, you wouldn't find them so funny."

He thumped his coffee mug onto the table and stormed out of the room. Liz, tempted to toss the coffeepot after him, heard the front door slam.

"Good riddance!" Sadie waved an arm. "All together now, hip-hip, hooray! Hip-hip, hooray! Hip-hip, hooray!"

Though fireworks still glowed in the angry women's eyes, they couldn't help giggling. By the time they had finished breakfast, all had left to explore Pleasant Creek in a positive mood.

Liz didn't know whether to thank Sadie for her offbeat management of the situation or to warn her not to tell Amish jokes.

As Sadie wouldn't listen anyway, she decided to thank her.

Sadie flexed her muscles. "When you want that guy thrown out for good, let me know."

"I'll bake him a pie." Mary Ann popped her head out the door of Sew Welcome. "One that tastes really bad."

Liz smiled. "I don't think that's possible." After her tenants returned to their store, she took out the trash. She also took out her frustrations on the back screen door, slamming it louder than necessary. While she cleared dishes, she formulated a Peabody Plan. She itched to let Mary Ann and Sadie wreak vengeance but saw the danger in setting that precedent for future grouchy clients. When Peabody returned, she would warn him that any additional rudeness would result in his immediate eviction.

After finishing cleaning the kitchen, Liz hurried upstairs to help Sarah tidy guest rooms. Though she liked the simple, contemporary decor of the Sunset Room, Peabody's earlier presence in it seemed to have grayed the room's cheerful colors. She finished her work in the room as quickly as possible. The quirky Somewhere in Time suite, with its eclectic collection of clocks, couldn't help but bring a smile to her lips. Walking into the Rose of Sharon room, she admired its flowery quilts, white vintage furniture—including a French armoire—and the bouquet of fuchsia tulips Kiera had arranged in a china pitcher that completed the magic. As Liz tucked lace-trimmed sheets and plumped pillows, she rehearsed her stern Peabody speech. While she and Sarah painted the last unfinished bedroom that afternoon, she polished her oration to perfection. Even unspoken, the words tasted good. She could hardly wait to deliver them, Lawyer Liz style.

But Peabody did not appear for coffee-and-cookie hour, thwarting her plans. *I should have known, after he pitched such a fit this morning.*

Nor did she see him when she briefly joined the other guests gathered at the gazebo to watch the sun set over Jaynes Lake. Earlier in the day, Sadie had taken the Louisville group to visit an Amish master quilter. Upon returning after supper, they had joined Emily, who'd opted for a lazy afternoon of reading and sunbathing on a nearby pier.

As if sun rays could penetrate all that fabric. Liz grinned. Carrying paint and gooey brushes between the inn and the garage, she'd seen Emily lying on the pier, covered with the floor-length terry-cloth robe she now wore, along with a floppy orange-and-lime polka-dotted hat—one Sadie would love.

A good hostess made her guests comfortable, but didn't linger too long. Having ensured the conversation was flowing, Liz excused herself, slipping away from the gazebo to a bench surrounded by delicious-smelling lilacs. Briefly she wondered when Mr. Peabody would return. Would he ring the doorbell in the wee hours, waking everyone? Liz attempted to massage irritation from her tight temples.

What if he'd stormed out of town and gone home?

She had to admit that she hoped so. Peabody had already paid for his two-night stay. If he'd left for Evansville early, she certainly wouldn't cry.

Stretching her shoulders, Liz focused on her private view: silhouetted, lacy trees and blazing pink sky and water, as if God had set thousands of roses on fire. Her pulse slowed to the evening's serene rhythm. Shifting on the bench, she pretended to make room for her mother to join her.

An easy first day? No. But overall, a good one. She gave thanks to God for bringing her to Pleasant Creek and asked Him again to help her find her family.

"Ms. Eckardt?"

The male voice, calling from the side yard, didn't sound like Peabody. Still Liz responded, "I'm in the backyard."

A moment later, two policemen emerged from the shadows, another guy trailing them in the twilight. Liz swallowed and stood. "May I help you?"

The older officer touched his hat. "I hope so, ma'am. Did Clarence Peabody stay here last night?"

"Yes. I'm expecting him back this evening too."

"I'm afraid that won't happen." The deep tone sounded vaguely familiar. Jackson Cross stepped from the shadows. "This evening, a fisherman found Peabody in the lake. Dead."

"Oh." Liz tried to clear her suddenly fogged brain. "Did he drown?"

Sadie's earlier joke about Amish water-skiing now took on a bizarre cast.

"Can't say for sure, yet." The older officer fixed her with a grim gaze. "However, I suspect that accidental drowning was not the cause of Mr. Peabody's death."

"Why do you say that?"

"There was a knife in his chest."

"Ms. Eckardt, would you like to sit down?"

The policeman's words echoed through Liz's head as if he had yelled them from far away and down a metal hallway. "All right."

A masculine hand gently guided her back to the bench. The lilacs' fragrance swirled around her like that of her mother's funeral flowers.

Jackson Cross said, "I'm so sorry this happened."

"So am I." The last feathery whorls of rose and gold still glistened in the sky, reflected in the lake. *How could such violence take place here—perhaps even as I and the other guests admired the sunset?*

Jackson faded into the dimness as the older policeman sat beside her. "I wish I didn't have to question you, ma'am, but I do."

"That's okay." She sucked in a quivering breath. "I want to help in any way I can."

He swiped his smartphone to take notes, and Liz set her mind on auto-lawyer.

In answering his questions, she offered scraps of information Clarence Peabody had spewed. He'd seemed upset throughout his stay. She knew nothing about his whereabouts after breakfast.

She recited what she knew about the other guests' backgrounds and activities. "The ladies all went out for lunch together after a morning of exploring the town. When they returned, they told me none planned to be here at the inn for coffee hour. Sadie Schwarzentruber took the Louisville group to visit an Amish quilter. They said they planned to go out for supper afterward. Emily sunbathed on the pier all afternoon." Liz pointed. "It's a bit of a walk, but when the sun's up, I can see it from here. We all met at the gazebo to enjoy the sunset about an hour ago."

Liz retraced her own movements: breakfast, cleanup, lunch,

painting all afternoon with Sarah, preparing for the no-show coffee hour, supper, cleanup again, and then joining her guests at the gazebo.

Her tired mind ran its own commentary. Surely she was not a suspect? *Of course I am. I left a high-paying job in Boston so I could sink a boatload of money into a B&B in Pleasant Creek, Indiana. Why? To murder a building contractor from Evansville, of course.*

She hoped it sounded as absurd to the police as it did to her.

Yet given Clarence's irascible personality, anyone who'd encountered him might be considered a suspect.

He's dead, her conscience reproached her, *and you're thinking this way?*

Somehow, she still expected Peabody to show up, barking about all of the hubbub.

Liz jumped when soft, warm arms enfolded her from behind, though she instinctively knew Mary Ann stood there.

"We're here for you, Liz."

She and Sadie sat down on opposite sides of Liz. For once, she *could* have gotten a word in edgewise.

But no one needed to say anything at all.

Why did the officer have to choose the living room to question everyone? Liz had never pictured the fireplace and cushy sofas as the scene of an interrogation.

Just yesterday, they'd eaten cookies here, talking and laughing like old friends. Now her guests sat upright as if attending a wake, with only an occasional murmur. The murder had even subdued Mary Ann and Sadie, who supplied whispered assurances and comforting pats to the gathered women.

Liz's mother's childhood portrait smiled from the mantel, so innocent, so untouched by evil. *Oh, Mom, if only you were here.*

But even her mother's presence could not undo the murder. Liz ached to call her godson, Steve, to hear his deep voice assure her that everything would be all right. But Steve was on a mission. She couldn't even email him. Sighing, she joined the group, longing to stretch her weary self out on a settee.

The stocky, gray-haired policeman who had interviewed Liz outside entered the room and greeted them. "I'm Stan Houghton, the department chief. Thanks for meeting with me."

As if we had a choice?

Liz quickly chided herself. The man was only doing his job. So far, he'd kept his approach reasonable and low-key. "Would you like coffee or tea, Chief Houghton?" she asked politely.

"No, thanks. I'll ask my questions and get out of your hair." His fatherly smile warmed Liz and then faded as his glance swept the room. "I'd appreciate whatever help you all can give in finding out who killed Mr. Peabody."

"We want to do everything we can to find that murderer," Mary Ann said, determination in her voice.

Nodding, the chief swiped his phone's screen with his finger. "First, did any of you know Mr. Peabody before his arrival yesterday?"

Emphatic noes sounded from all the women. Sadie added a "thank goodness."

"Did you talk with him while he was here, learn anything about him?"

"A little at breakfast this morning," Helen said in her ladylike Kentucky drawl. "He didn't seem much inclined toward conversation—"

"Not with us, anyway." Violet shrugged. "He seemed mad at the world."

"Especially the Amish," Vera, her twin, chimed in. "Said something about knowing them better than we did."

Emily nodded. "He did say that."

Houghton asked each guest about contact information, background, and reasons for visiting Pleasant Creek.

As the questioning continued, Liz's respect for Houghton grew. This small-town police chief possessed a gift for probing without antagonizing his subjects.

He said, "I know you've been here only a day or so, but did anything strike you as unusual?"

The quilters shook their heads again, but Liz noticed that Emily looked at her hands.

"Ms. Hart?" The chief injected a cajoling note into his voice. "Please tell me whatever came to mind, no matter how unimportant it might seem."

Pushing at one cuticle and then another, Emily raised dark eyes to meet his gaze. "I-I don't want to cause anyone trouble."

"Of course you don't." Houghton leaned toward her. "But you want to help us catch the person who killed Mr. Peabody, don't you?"

Emily exhaled and nodded. "I don't know if this has anything to do with anything. But this afternoon, as I was sunbathing on the pier, I stood to stretch and saw . . . I saw . . ."

"What did you see, Ms. Hart?" No coaxing now. The chief demanded an answer.

"A young man in Amish dress, perhaps twenty or so. He ran past me." The words whooshed from the woman like air from a balloon.

"Did you see his face? Would you recognize him?"

"Yes." She raised her quivering chin. "He looked frightened."

"Thank you for telling me." Houghton gave Emily's arm a fatherly pat, which seemed to calm her. "Let's talk further about this—perhaps in a different room?" He shot a questioning glance at Liz.

Liz rose. "Uh, yes. You may use my personal sitting room." Over the past few weeks, she'd invested all of her energy in making the guest areas of the inn beautiful, and her private quarter's near-squalor had seemed unimportant. Now she wished she'd paid a little more attention to the mess that would greet the chief and her guest.

"Thank you all for your help." Chief Houghton nodded a dismissal.

"I'm sure you're anxious to leave this incident behind, but as a routine precaution, could you all remain in our area for a day or two?"

Liz held her breath as the women exchanged looks. She had counted on their four-day stay—and those of future guests to this lovely, safe little town . . .

"Let's stay." Violet's button mouth flattened into a firm line. "We shouldn't let this scare us off. I still want to go to the Quilters Hall of Fame in Marion tomorrow with Mary Ann."

Vera nodded. "We already bought tickets for the Tuesday buggy ride too."

"Great." The chief edged Emily toward the door, motioning for Liz to lead on.

As they trudged to her apartment located down a short hall off the kitchen, Liz recalled her earlier hopes that her first days as an innkeeper would prove memorable.

Definitely.

She would never forget this day as long as she lived.

Bustling to put breakfast on the table the next morning, Liz stopped short as Sarah entered, easing the screen door closed in silence. Liz set down a tray of fruit cups. "Are you still feeling sick?"

Liz had sent the girl home early the previous afternoon because she looked ill. This morning, she still drooped, and her rosy cheeks had paled.

"I'm just a little tired." Sarah retied her already perfect apron bow.

"If you need to go home, I'll take you."

"I'm fine."

Sarah didn't look fine, but she didn't look compliant either, and Liz did need the help. "All right. I suppose our main goal is to simply to make it through the day without any additional drama." Liz hesitated. "Perhaps you heard about Mr. Peabody—"

"*Ja*. How horrible." The girl slipped past her. "Should I work in the Heirloom Room until you need me to clear up breakfast?"

"Yes, the paint's probably dry—"

Sarah vanished upstairs.

Liz blinked. Someone banged on the back door.

It was Chief Houghton. "Morning, Ms. Eckardt." He smiled ruefully. "'Good morning' doesn't really fit, does it?"

She tried to smile too. "What can I do for you?"

"I need to talk to anyone else you can think of who's been around the Olde Mansion Inn the past few days. Employees, for instance."

Great. "I have two employees. Sarah Yoder, who's working upstairs right now, and Kiera Williams. She comes in about three o'clock. I'm not sure she even saw Peabody though."

"Still, I need to talk to everyone. May I borrow your sitting room again to interview Sarah?"

"Of course." Liz brushed back a limp strand of hair. "Make yourself at home. I'll bring her right in." She felt it was better that she, rather than the chief, approach the skittish girl first.

Even a few minutes of work seemed to have energized Sarah. Though still pale, she entered Liz's quarters with her back straight and shoulders squared. Within fifteen minutes, Liz saw her exit, still appearing composed, and return upstairs. Liz breathed a sigh of relief as she placed a maple-sausage bread pudding in front of eager diners.

A moment later, the chief appeared in the foyer. Liz slipped away from the dining room long enough to whisper, "Sarah's feeling ill, but she wouldn't go home. Thanks for dealing with her so well."

Chief Houghton matched her low tone. "I expected her to be upset. The Amish hate violence, and they really dislike talking with the police." He ushered her inside the apartment door. "Do you remember seeing anyone else—familiar or unfamiliar—on the premises these past couple of weeks?"

Liz named off the Material Girls and then counted on her fingers.

"The mailman. The UPS guy. Calvin the carpenter—Mary Ann's friend who built shelves in their shop. I don't know his last name." No repairmen. She'd solved the most recent plumbing problem herself. "Miriam Borkholder and her girls, and other customers came to Sew Welcome before it officially opened. Mary Ann and Sadie seemed to know all of them well. I think that's everyone."

He thanked her and left to reexamine the crime scene. With his exit, Mary Ann and Sadie exploded through the front door. They seemed to have recovered well from their temporary quietude. Opal eased inside behind them and gave Liz a sympathetic smile.

"We'll take turns helping you today." Sadie, wearing old jeans and a T-shirt, raised a caddy of cleaning supplies. "Opal and I will take first shift. Just point us in the right direction, and we'll do the inn proud."

Liz protested, "Thanks, but that's not necess—"

"Of course, it is. You've got a lot on your mind." Sadie started up the stairs.

"We Material Girls don't just sew together. We help each other." Opal patted Liz's shoulder and followed Sadie.

So much for pointing anyone in the right direction. *Maybe they're right.* Liz's footsteps dragged as if she'd run a marathon the day before.

"I'll be in Sew Welcome if you need me." Mary Ann gestured at the picnic basket she'd set down. "But first, tell me where to put these pies."

"I'll take them to the pantry," Liz said. Judging by the weight of the basket, Mary Ann must have baked at least four. A thin smile touched Liz's lips even as her arm muscles ached. Did the woman believe plying the globe with pie could achieve world peace?

"You'd better have some right away." Mary Ann shook her pink-nailed finger in Liz's face. "I think the blueberry is best, but my shoofly pie matches up pretty close to the Amish version, if I do say so myself."

Liz's taste buds awakened, if nothing else did. She lugged the basket into the pantry and cut big wedges from the recommended pies, now keenly aware she'd skipped breakfast in order to cook for her guests. She'd never tasted shoofly pie. Curiosity sent a bite of the crumbly topped, rich-looking pie into her mouth.

Oh.

More followed. Then she had a piece of blueberry pie. *Maybe Mary Ann's pies could achieve world peace after all . . .*

Paired with strong coffee, the impromptu feast fueled her body and soul. As Liz mounted the stairs, Sadie's slightly off-key rendition of the 1950s hit *Splish Splash* floated from a guest bathroom. Liz poked her head in the room. A dervish of pine-scented energy, Sadie boogied as she cleaned every inch from toilet to tub. Opal was busy dusting the tops of the tall windows with a dry mop, eyeing the ceiling as if daring a spiderweb to appear. Chuckling, Liz headed for the next bedroom where dust mop thumps and bumps confirmed Sarah's presence.

The matching knots in Liz's left shoulder and stomach began to loosen. Maybe she *would* make it through this day without any more . . . problems.

"Liz!" Emily's voice rang out from the first floor. "I hate to bother you, but the downstairs restroom is, um, malfunctioning. I'm afraid the kitchen sink is clogged too."

Liz's fledging optimism vanished. So much for self-repair and money saved.

"Be there in a moment." She flew to the rescue, pulling her cell phone from her pocket. For the next several hours, her world revolved around pipes, drains, and mounting bills. Mercifully, the Louisville guests were spending the day elsewhere.

But as news of the murder spread, the citizens of Pleasant Creek suddenly discovered an immediate need for quilting patterns, fabric, and embroidery floss. Cars filled the inn's small parking lot. Townspeople, farmers, and even some Amish visitors wandered the inn and its grounds.

Liz had aspired to run a relaxed bed-and-breakfast—not a Midwestern Grand Central Station.

A laid-back atmosphere? Hardly.

At least one of the inn's regulars seemed unperturbed by yesterday's events: Beans sprawled on his—and Liz's—favorite rug near the front door. He stared at her, however, with a particularly dour expression, as if the chaos that was interrupting his sleep was all her fault.

She escaped to Sew Welcome's back room and told Mary Ann and Sadie that her business didn't need this kind of publicity.

"Certainly, you'd never want it. But it may work in your favor." Mary Ann gestured at a guestbook on the foyer desk. "I'm having everyone sign in as they enter, in case the police want to know who came in today."

Liz nodded numbly. That record would not include the dozens of people swarming the lake paths, but why not? She slipped past chattering visitors and headed toward the kitchen, where the plumber was finishing. She should have eaten lunch hours ago. But maybe she'd make another meal out of pie. Too bad nothing remained of the shoofly but crumbs. Right now, she could have eaten the whole thing.

"Ms. Eckardt?"

So many people had tugged on her elbow over the past twenty-four hours. *This must be how a kindergarten teacher feels*. Liz turned to see a young man with keen brown eyes staring at her. "Yes?"

"I'm with the *Indianapolis Gazette*. I'm covering the Clarence Peabody murder—"

"And I'm with the *Fort Wayne Times*." A power-suited blonde stood at Liz's other elbow.

"Would you care to make a statement?" they chorused in perfect unison and then glared at each other.

Liz fled—away from people and away from questions. She ran to her sitting room and plopped down on the sofa. But soon a *tap-tap-tap* sounded on her door.

She buried her head under a throw pillow.

The taps turned to knocks. Louder knocks.

"I don't want to make a statement!" she shouted.

Silence. Then, "Miss Eckardt?"

Sarah.

Liz leaped to the door and opened it. She suppressed a gasp. If Sarah had looked sickly this morning, she resembled a corpse now. Liz slipped an arm around the girl. "Tell me what's wrong and how I can help."

Rivulets of tears ran down Sarah's face. "No one can help us. No one but *Gött.*"

Help "us"? Liz drew the girl into her sitting room—an area screened off inside the inn's large first-floor bedroom. Tears still trickling, Sarah automatically brushed wasabi snack mix from the sofa and plumped pillows.

Liz smiled. "I'll pay you extra to clean up this mess later, but for now, just sit. All right?"

Dabbing at her eyes, the girl sat.

Liz took her hand. "What's on your mind?"

A fresh torrent of tears poured down Sarah's cheeks. "My cousin ate lunch with me. Oh, Miss Eckardt, she told me the police questioned Isaac about . . . about . . ."

"Mr. Peabody?" Liz asked gently. Sadie had teased Sarah about her young man, but this was the first time the quiet girl had mentioned his name.

"Isaac would never, never hurt anyone!" Sarah's wet face reddened, and her green eyes flashed. "Not even if Mr. Peabody had harmed him. That is not our way."

"Do you know what led the police to Isaac?"

"Someone boating on the lake recognized him as he was walking along the shore." Her shoulders slumped again.

Liz countered, "Isaac didn't know Mr. Peabody, did he?"

"No. Why would they question him?" She beat clenched fists softly on her thighs.

"Probably only a formality." Liz handed her a tissue. "They questioned many people, Sarah, including us."

A hint of hope lit Sarah's face as she brushed the tissue across her cheeks. "Ja. I suppose they have to talk to everyone. Even our bishop." The tinge of optimism faded to an intense look of distaste. "Mr. Peabody made a scene at his farm yesterday, shouting and threatening. Something ridiculous about the Amish causing his company's bankruptcy."

"Yet I don't imagine they suspect the bishop." Liz inserted a tiny edge of humor into her voice, though she stored this information for future ponderings.

"No." Sarah still twisted the edge of her apron, fresh tears streaming down her face. "But the officers talked to Isaac for almost two hours."

Liz summoned her best client-soothing voice. "When they investigate further, I'm sure they'll realize Isaac had no motive for attacking Mr. Peabody."

Though the girl's sobs diminished to sniffles, her jaw tightened.

Another rap on the door. Sarah sat up straight.

When Liz opened it, Chief Houghton and Kiera stood outside. "Hello." She blocked their view, giving Sarah time to wipe away her tears. "I see you have met Kiera?"

"Mary Ann introduced us," the chief said cheerfully.

Kiera looked as if she wished she were pulling weeds in the hot afternoon sun.

Liz didn't want to offer, but she stretched a smile across her face. "Do you need my sitting room again?"

"If you don't mind." The chief hastened to add, "Kiera's mother gave me permission to interview her. You can remain though—in fact, I'd appreciate your presence."

"Did you need to ask Sarah anything else?" With that question, Liz had thought to ease her maid out of the room. But glancing over her shoulder, she saw Sarah's eyes widen in terror.

Chief Houghton shook his head. "I don't think so."

His cell phone rang, and he barked monosyllables into it. Sarah popped up from the sofa and slipped behind Liz, allowing the others to pass through the door first. But while the chief talked, Liz intercepted a glance between the teens that made her catch her breath.

Sarah's icy glare froze the space between them. Kiera shot back a defiant arrow of a look.

Liz had never detected trouble between her employees before. What in the world was going on?

Liz wanted to dash after Sarah's retreating figure. *Is this just some teen drama? Or something more serious?*

However, having promised to remain for Kiera's interview, Liz retrieved her tablet and sat on the sofa, determined to listen carefully.

The chief ended his phone call, poising phone and fingers to take notes.

Kiera perched on her chair, but his comfortable manner seemed to ease her tense posture. They reviewed her whereabouts the day Peabody arrived. She had been weeding the front flower beds when he strode up the sidewalk "as if he owned the place," Kiera said. When she finished the day's tasks, she washed up in the potting shed sink before reporting to Liz that she was leaving.

"Did you see Mr. Peabody any time after that first arrival?" Chief Houghton asked.

Instead of the quick "no" Liz had expected, the girl hesitated a long minute. She tucked her pointed chin into her chest.

The chief said gently, "Kiera, it's important we trace every minute of Mr. Peabody's last hours."

Liz set her tablet aside. Kiera suddenly raised her head, jerking her words as if they were on leashes. "I was walking out of the potting shed when Mr. Peabody came out the inn's back door—"

"When was that?" the chief prompted.

"Thursday, two days ago. The same day he first came but maybe an hour later." Kiera continued, "Sarah was leaving the garage, carrying a bucket of paint."

Harmless words. But they moved Liz to stand at the girl's side.

"Go on." Chief Houghton didn't change expression.

"Sarah walked toward the house and waited for Mr. Peabody to pass her on the sidewalk so she could take the paint inside. But he stopped instead and asked if he could carry it for her." Kiera swallowed. "She said, 'No, thanks,' but he took it anyway and set it on the sidewalk. He . . . he touched Sarah's cheek. I guess she was too blown away to move, 'cause then he grabbed her and kissed her."

Nauseated, Liz fought to keep her composure. Apparently, Peabody didn't hate *all* Amish. No wonder Sarah had looked ill. Why hadn't she said anything?

The chief said calmly, "It wasn't like a father's kiss, right? Or an uncle's?"

"No way." Kiera rolled her eyes. "That gross old guy was putting the moves on her."

How dare he? Liz chewed her lip. *If the man weren't already dead, I'd hurt him.*

"How did Sarah react?" the chief's voice remained neutral.

"It was like she finally woke up. She jerked away and ran into the house."

Liz blurted, "Why didn't she tell me?"

"Her silence isn't surprising. The Amish are generally slow to make accusations." Shaking his head, the chief turned back to Kiera. "Thanks for answering honestly. Did you see Mr. Peabody any other time?"

"No. I'm glad I didn't."

Even Liz's turmoil couldn't keep a small smile away. Kiera always said what she thought. No more, no less.

"One more thing." The chief looked up from his phone. "Do you know Isaac Borkholder?"

Liz's mouth went dry. Was this Sarah's Isaac? If so, was he related to Miriam Borkholder, with whom she had felt such a kindred spirit? And why would Houghton ask Kiera about him?

"He's a few years older than you," the chief continued. "About twenty."

"Don't think so." Kiera raised a shoulder in a small shrug. "I may have seen him around town, but I've never met him."

After Kiera had left to mow and Chief Houghton had departed to reexamine the crime site for the umpteenth time, Liz practically ran to the kitchen. She grabbed a container of gourmet chocolate chip cookie dough from the fridge. There were only thirty minutes left before coffee-and-cookie hour, and given today's stresses, she thought she'd better bake two sheets. While she dipped, plopped, and baked, her mind tried to make sense of it all.

Mary Ann could confirm if Isaac Borkholder was related to Miriam. She also would know if this Isaac and Sarah's boyfriend were one and the same.

An anemic chuckle rose in Liz's throat. By now, Mary Ann probably knew more about the investigation than Chief Houghton did.

Beginning the second pan of cookies, Liz tried once more to analyze the sudden tension between Sarah and Kiera. Her employees had gotten along reasonably well before the Peabody incident. And a love triangle didn't make sense. The mention of Isaac during Kiera's interview hadn't sparked any obvious interest on her part. Given Sarah's reticence, Liz doubted she had even told Kiera she had a boyfriend, much less his name.

Perhaps the girls' conflict had arisen simply because Sarah wanted Kiera to keep quiet about Clarence Peabody's conduct. She might think Liz would blame her for the incident. Sarah also might fear her family's reaction if they found out, or the Amish community's.

Or Isaac's.

Liz's chest tightened. Sarah was right. The police evidently had considered him one of their more likely suspects, or Houghton would not have asked Kiera if she knew him.

Isaac had been seen close to the crime scene. But why would he kill an out-of-town "English" contractor? What would make a twenty-year-old Amish boy turn violent?

Peabody and Sarah.

Surely their unfortunate encounter was an isolated incident. But what if Isaac believed otherwise?

Kiera had just supplied Isaac with a motive for killing Peabody—and Sarah's big reason for hiding the "let me carry your paint" incident.

Would Houghton think the evidence against Isaac was sufficient to arrest him?

Liz closed her eyes. If only Clarence Peabody had never darkened her inn's doorstep.

A hundred despairing possibilities flapped around her. She sank into a kitchen chair, unable to fight them off, until the smell of burning cookies catapulted her into action.

An emergency phone order to Naomi's bakery next door helped Liz survive cookie-and-coffee hour, during which she answered guests' questions and allayed fears as best she could. She'd managed a veneer of politeness when reporters and TV personnel invaded their social time and helped themselves to refreshments.

We need all the positive press we can get.

One tripped over Beans, sprawling headlong. Liz, visualizing shattered limbs and lawsuits, tried to help the very large man get up. He waved her aside and pushed himself to a sitting position, rubbing his nose and laughing. "That old bulldog hasn't moved a hair. Are you sure he's got a heartbeat?"

After they left, Liz zoomed back to the living room to clean up. A large, dark stain had blossomed on the carpet under the coffee table. *Blast.* She sopped up spilled coffee.

"You call this a simpler life?"

Oh, no. Hoping she'd finally gone over the edge and was hearing imaginary voices, Liz straightened. She didn't want to turn around.

"You *could* at least say 'hello.'" The man's voice drawled.

Slowly, she turned and faced him.

Matt Sheridan, her ex-boyfriend, draped his long, sleek frame across the sofa. He was a reporter, not an actor. Why did he treat every moment as a photo op? "What are you doing here? Trying to get the scoop?"

"Of course." His gaze fell below her comfort level. "For an innkeeper, you're not very hospitable." He still had the same maddening smile. He was magazine-cover attractive and just about as sincere.

Liz crossed her arms. "I don't recall issuing you an invitation."

"Do all your guests receive invitations?"

"Matt, I'm not in the mood to play games—"

"I'm not surprised." His smile didn't falter, but he crossed his arms too. "Murder does that to people. News flash, honey: Indiana isn't the perfect little place you thought it would be."

"Crime happens everywhere."

"But some guy was stabbed in your own backyard, literally. How's that going to affect your business?"

"Technically, the man was found on the *far* side of the lake. And my business is none of your business." *How well we fight—as if we've memorized a script.* Suddenly weary, she said, "Matt, I won't quarrel with you today. We can't agree on anything. You know that. I know that. So let's try to be civil, wish each other well, and say goodbye again. For real. Forever."

"This murder business has gotten to you more than you think." He rose from the sofa. "Liz, I'm worried about you. You look so tired."

"I am tired. Tired of this." She pushed away his hand.

"Let me take you somewhere to rest. Somewhere special."

He'd emailed her resort pictures right before their breakup, pictures that now popped up in her mind as if he'd hit a button. "Stop it, Matt. I never went on trips with you when we were together. I'm certainly not going now."

"Think Hawaii. Or an Alaskan cruise. I know of a quiet little town just outside Paris—"

"Paris? You can't go to Paris!" Sadie exclaimed, poking her flowery-floppy-hatted head between them. "Or anyplace else. I just lined up all 187 of my relatives to stay at the inn between now and New Year's."

Liz had never seen her ex speechless. Matt, who had a gibe, a jive, and a lie handy at all times, stared, his mouth moving silently like a guppy's.

Laughter bubbled into Liz's throat, bursting out her nose. She tried to cover her snort with a cough.

"Of course, she can't go anywhere." Mary Ann moved in for the kill, teeth shining like a shark's. She took Matt's left elbow, Sadie grabbed the right, and together they edged him toward the door. "We love Liz way too much," Mary Ann crooned. "So you go back to the city, son, where you belong."

Liz didn't follow, but she heard Matt sputter, "What is this? Who *are* you people? You have no right!"

Grrrrrr.

Liz sucked in a breath. *It can't be.* She bounded into the foyer.

It is! Beans stood—actually stood!—inches away from Matt's ankles. His bared teeth looked nowhere near as pretty as Mary Ann's, but they looked sharper. *Grrrrrrrrrr.*

"Get that dog away from me!" Matt squeaked.

"But Beans is such a nice puppy," Sadie cooed, pushing Matt closer to the enraged bulldog. Beans bellowed, rather than barked, and Matt sprinted across the foyer and right out the door, the dog snapping at his heels as he went.

Liz gave up concealing her giggles. She laughed so hard her stomach ached, her face ached, and she felt better than she had in weeks.

"Nice-looking guy." Sadie watched Matt peel out of the parking lot. "But a good-looking skunk still stinks."

"You are so right." Liz hugged both of her "bodyguards." Then she knelt by Beans, who had dropped back onto his rug like a sack of sand. She gave his ears a thorough scratch. He groaned with happiness.

"Beans *is* a nice puppy," she crooned, Sadie-style. "He got rid of that good-for-nothing guy, didn't he?"

Beans simply closed his eyes and began to snore.

Sadie burst through the inn's back door. "The divers think they found the *real* murder weapon!" She'd been providing unsolicited play-by-play reports all morning.

Now Liz, en route to the laundry room, froze, a basket of dirty towels clasped to her stomach. "I thought we already knew it was a knife?"

"Just come on!" Sadie gestured impatiently.

I don't want to see it—whatever it is. Liz's stomach objected to the whole scenario.

But Sadie dragged her to the lakeshore, where a small crowd of divers, officers, reporters, and curiosity seekers had gathered.

"It was an awl that did him in," Sadie intoned with an anchorwoman's drama. "*Not* the knife"

Liz thought the knife probably hadn't helped. "How do you know this?"

Sadie merely shrugged.

Liz had steered away from criminal law to avoid sordid details like these. She never imagined she'd one day encounter them behind her house. Why had she let Sadie drag her outside? Even if she'd wanted to see the awl, surely it now resided in an evidence bag.

"They wouldn't let me look at it up close," Sadie groused as the parade of participants passed and headed for their cars, "but I saw it. I heard a policemen say they were going to test it for fingerprints. Of course, they'd have to. Every Amish man in the county owns one." For the first time, a hint of worry clouded Sadie's voice. "It's almost as if someone's trying to make it look like one of them murdered Peabody."

In a low voice, Liz said, "I heard that the police questioned a young man named Isaac Borkholder."

"They can question all they want." Sadie sniffed. "Isaac is Miriam's oldest. He's a good boy who wouldn't hurt a fly."

Now Liz's stomach roiled. She'd so hoped he was one of the gazillion anonymous Borkholders on the property tax list.

Sadie's eyes sparked. "It's a crying shame they're upsetting him and his family over this. Just because Isaac happened to be walking near the lake around five—I heard a policeman give that as the time of the murder." She crossed her arms. "Sarah's upset too. Everybody's been waiting to hear they're engaged."

So Liz had been right on both counts. Sadie fell silent as they walked back to the inn.

I can't let this horrible murder take over my life. We can't let it take over everyone's lives. Liz straightened her shoulders and forced a smile. "I've been thinking. With all this trouble, we need a pick-me-up. Would you and Mary Ann be willing to hold a quilting class before our Louisville group leaves?"

"That's a great idea." Sadie beamed. "The Material Girls were supposed to meet soon, anyway, to work on our fall quilt. Anything on your schedule tomorrow evening?"

"No." Liz had hoped to study her mother's diary, but the guests needed a cheerful end to their so-called vacation. "You talk to Mary Ann, and I'll check with Violet and company. Emily too. When our new couple checks in this afternoon, I'll invite them. "

Naturally, Mary Ann jumped at the idea. "Let's have a potluck beforehand!"

The guests, having returned after lunch, voted yes. "We were hoping to do something all together," Vera enthused.

The plan returned the sparkle to everyone's eyes—except Sarah's. Paler and quieter than ever, she declined to participate.

At Liz's invitation, Kiera's face lit up. But almost as quickly, her eagerness faded. "I sewed at school, but that's all I've ever done."

"This is the perfect chance to check out quilting."

The girl hemmed and hawed. Liz pressed, "I had really hoped you and Sarah could come—"

"Sarah isn't coming?" Kiera jumped on that detail too quickly.

Liz pretended not to notice. "Tomorrow isn't good for her."

"I-I think I can come." The teen's eyes brightened.

"Don't worry about bringing sewing stuff or food. With Mary Ann and Sadie taking charge, there'll be plenty of both."

Even the discovery of the murder weapon didn't undermine the air of anticipation in the Olde Mansion Inn.

Their potluck—in reality, a feast—particularly delighted Jim Baylor, who, along with wife, Marge, had accepted Liz's invitation at check-in the day before. "I told her we shouldn't let a few TV newscasts delay our trip to Pleasant Creek." The silver-haired man helped himself to thirds of Sadie's chicken and noodles. "Look what we would have missed!"

"It is wonderful"—Marge rolled dark, mascaraed eyes—"but I'm sure there's more to Amish country than just food."

"Lots more!" Emily exclaimed.

The other guests and the Material Girls steered the conversation far away from newscasts and toward Pleasant Creek's sights.

After pitching in to clean up, they adjourned to Sew Welcome's airy, many-windowed workroom. Liz realized that with all the chaos, she'd taken little time to explore her friends' craft. Now, as Naomi unfolded the Material Girls' fall quilt, Liz echoed her guests' delight as they gathered around the long table. The partially finished quilt featured a maple leaf pattern repeated in brilliant autumn gold, scarlet, and melon solids and prints, scattered artistically among dark green, chocolate, and russet rectangles.

"We want to complete it for the county's October auction," Naomi said. "We hope it will help fund next year's projects."

Jim had excused himself to take a walk, but Marge's gaze never left the quilt.

She'll show up for the auction. Mentally saving her pennies, Liz added a reminder to her phone as well.

"I'd better get to cutting." Opal's scissors skimmed skillfully through fabrics.

Caitlyn took Kiera under her wing, showing her which fabric pieces to pin together where. Marge, who had attended some quilting classes, joined Emily, Violet, and Liz at four sewing machines, piecing points and rectangles. Naomi and Sadie pressed, assembled, and sewed the others' work together, while Mary Ann, Vera, Jill, and Helen embroidered stems on completed leaf blocks.

Sadie peered at the growing piles of pieces Opal had cut. "I guess you're keeping up. You're not half bad, old lady."

"I'm way ahead, and you know it." Opal withered her with a look. "If you're so good, you come over here and cut."

Sadie's eyes glinted. "I would, if you didn't hog the best scissors."

"Don't mind them." Grinning, Mary Ann rolled her eyes. "They've been feuding ever since the 1960 county fair—"

"I deserved the grand champion ribbon for my apron. It was perfect, with yellow daisies." Sadie's wistful smile at the memory flipped to a frown, and she glared at Opal. "But the judge was your second cousin."

A wicked smile materialized on Opal's prim face and then vanished so fast Liz almost missed it. "I won, fair and square."

"No, you didn't!"

"Sew with us a couple more times and you'll know that script by heart." Naomi chuckled as the two scrapped.

Their banter reminded Liz of the perfect horseradish sauce she hoped to master for a future pot roast—enough zing to keep things interesting, leaving behind a warm, pleasantly spicy aura.

It was exactly the effect she'd desired this evening. Grinning at the pair's jibes, everyone talked and sewed. Between arguments and sewing, Sadie took pictures. Emily, as well as Caitlyn, reached out to Kiera.

The only iffy spot in the evening was Sadie's avoidance of Emily.

She chatted to everyone but the librarian, not answering her questions, not laughing at her stories.

What is that about? How had Emily offended Liz's lovable but fiery tenant? Had her guest taken Opal's side during the great apron debate? At least Sadie hadn't aimed any barbs at Emily.

Liz breathed a sigh of relief at evening's end. Mary Ann thanked everyone, predicting that despite summer schedules, the Material Girls would achieve their October goal.

After everyone scattered, Liz hummed as she began preparations for the next morning's breakfast. She glanced out the window realizing she'd missed the sunset's carnival colors. Perhaps the brilliant hues of tomorrow's sunrise would make up for it. When she let Beans out, she'd watch the dawn highlight the clock tower's silhouette.

The next day dawned as beautifully as she'd hoped. Her new spinach-and-mushroom quiche recipe cooperated, generating fervent compliments from the Kentucky quilters, reluctantly finishing their farewell breakfast. Everyone hugged everyone else goodbye and promised to look for each other on the social networking sites.

All was well in Pleasant Creek and the world.

It was, that is, until Mary Ann and Sadie arrived, whispering the news that Isaac Borkholder had been arrested for the murder of Clarence Peabody.

7

Arrested? Why had paralysis suddenly struck Liz's mind and body? She'd never met Isaac. Still, some evil gravity riveted her to the hallway's wide-planked floor.

"They took him to jail last night." For once, Mary Ann's smile had abandoned her. Her usually vibrant skin had paled.

Sadie looked like a summer thunderstorm ready to erupt.

Liz forced her mouth to move. "I'll come to Sew Welcome after the Kentucky guests leave."

Despite the murder's horrific impact, she really had enjoyed hosting the ladies. Liz helped Helen, Violet, Vera, and Jill carry their luggage to their SUV, aided by Emily, almost a member of the club. She and Jill, in particular, had seemed to connect.

The Louisville bunch planned to return within the year. "Next time, we'll bring more quilting-club members," Helen assured Liz.

"We had a wonderful time." Jill patted her shoulder. "It wasn't your fault that disagreeable old man died."

Liz clung to their positive comments. She and Emily returned to the dining room to find Mary Ann and Sadie cleaning up.

She welcomed the assistance, especially because Sarah, for the first time, was late. But as Emily gathered plates, Liz tapped her on the shoulder. "Hey, the last time I checked, you're a guest here."

"I've been incredibly lazy." The librarian smiled. "I can lift a dish or two."

Her helpfulness, however, only seemed to darken Sadie's ongoing sulk. When Emily said she was leaving for Indianapolis for the day, Liz exhaled. Right now, she didn't want to deal with Sadie's weirdness and the tension it brought.

After scrubbing gooey pans, she coaxed her feet to take her to Sew Welcome. Thankfully, Sadie was waiting on customers. Mary Ann motioned Liz to the workroom.

Liz fingered the fall quilt, stowed in one of the large wall cubbyholes. Only last night, they'd had such fun here! "How did you find out about Isaac?"

"I heard rumors this morning at the café, so I went to Miriam's." Mary Anne's dark brown eyes swam with tears. "She's heartbroken."

Thinking of her own godson, Liz couldn't imagine Miriam's pain. Had Kiera's interview with Chief Houghton brought about Isaac's arrest? Liz gulped. "Have the police found new evidence?"

"The fingerprint tests from the awl came back. They're Isaac's. Only Isaac's." Mary Ann said, shaking her head. "The police think he ran into Peabody while taking a walk around the lake, argued with him about his harassing Sarah, and stabbed him. I never would have believed it of Isaac. Not in the worst of circumstances."

Liz sighed. "I can't imagine how Sarah's feeling."

"She's devastated." Mary Ann opened a drawer. Her deft fingers began arranging and rearranging notions. "I stopped by her house and told her to take the morning off. Still she insisted she would come this afternoon."

Sympathy for Sarah's plight overruled Liz's spike of annoyance at finding that once more she was the junior partner in her one-woman business. But her lawyer's mind fiddled with a detail that didn't fit. "If Isaac committed the murder on impulse, why would he be carrying an awl?"

"Good question." Mary Ann jammed pins into defenseless cushions and then raised her gaze to meet Liz's. She said slowly, "What if . . . what if Isaac didn't do it impulsively?"

Pain seeped from Mary Ann's every word.

"You mean, what if he planned the murder?" Liz recoiled, but shook her head. "That doesn't make sense weapon-wise either. If an

Amish man were bent on murder, why would he use an awl—something closely associated with his community?"

"I certainly don't know where Isaac would find a switchblade." A mirthless smile tugged at Mary Ann's mouth. "But it does seem he'd use something else—a weapon that wouldn't point straight to him."

"Switchblades, butcher knives, awls. I don't care what anybody says." Sadie's voice, like a bugle, made Liz jump. "Isaac didn't do it."

"We don't think so either, Sadie." Liz touched her arm. "We're just trying to look at things objectively—"

"I'll tell you who *did* do it." Sadie crossed her arms like rapiers.

Liz blinked. How could Sadie possibly know who killed Clarence Peabody? Had she seen or heard something no one else had?

"Now, Sadie," Mary Ann soothed, but she edged across the workroom toward the shop door.

"Don't worry. The customers are gone." Sadie stuck out her chin. "It was that sneaky librarian."

Liz felt her jaw unhinge. "Emily?"

"We've talked about this before, Sadie." Mary Ann sounded like a third-grade teacher. "There is absolutely no reason to suspect Emily. The police would have pursued her if there was."

"She's pretending to be so sweet and *helpful.*" Sadie spat the last word like an expletive. "But I know she isn't."

Liz said carefully, "You noticed something that gave you that impression?"

"It's not an impression. I *know.*" Sadie grabbed her red hat with the orange and purple flowers off a wall hook, stuck it on her head, and glared at Mary Ann. "If I'm watching the shop this afternoon while you go to the funeral, I'm taking the rest of the morning off."

"That's fine, dear—"

Sadie slammed the door, setting off a *rat-tat-tat* of all the room's glass and plastic containers.

Liz said lamely, "I'm sorry I upset her."

Mary Ann sighed. "Sadie does understand people in a unique, intuitive way. But once in a while she gets something bizarre stuck in her head, and it completely takes over." She rolled her eyes heavenward.

"What can we do to calm her?" Liz really, really did not need more excitement around the inn, and Emily was staying two more days.

"Oh, she'll calm herself. Give her an hour of riding her tractor and she'll be fine. Well, until something else sets her off."

Liz fiddled with thimbles in a carved box. Until then, would she and Mary Ann walk a minefield? "What was that about a funeral?"

Mary Ann sliced open a box UPS had delivered that morning. Her hands blurred as she retrieved and folded fabric. "I heard Tom is burying Clarence Peabody this afternoon."

"Tom?" Liz asked. "Is he Peabody's relative?"

"No, Tom Yoder is Pleasant Creek's funeral director, a high school classmate of mine. His family has run Yoder's Funeral Home for generations." Mary Ann clucked her tongue. "It's sad. The police finally tracked down Clarence's brother, Gene, for an official identification of the body. Gene arranged for a graveside service at 1:30 today."

Liz had hoped to avoid funerals the rest of her life. But she raised her chin. "I'm going too. I feel—not exactly responsible for Mr. Peabody—but he was my guest. I want to express sympathy to his brother. From what you say, I doubt many will attend the service." She paused. "I also might learn something that could shed new light on Clarence's killing. If there's anything I can do to help Isaac, I'd like to."

"Let's go together." Mary Ann flapped the final piece of fabric into a perfect rectangle. "At the very least, Gene Peabody will know Pleasant Creek is a town that cares, even if he finds that hard to believe right now."

Did the glorious May day intend to insult Clarence Peabody's dubious legacy and tragic death, or was it trying to make the best of a terrible situation? Liz chose to believe the latter.

"Much better to have the service outdoors," Mary Ann said as Liz parked her Acura along a narrow cemetery road. "I like Tom, but I hope he replaces that terrible, splashy carpet at the funeral home before I die."

"Good afternoon, ladies." Jackson Cross, wearing a dark sport coat, joined them as they walked toward the gravesite.

Echoing his greeting, Liz's estimation of the man rose. Jackson, as mayor, probably shared her sense of obligation to Clarence Peabody and his relatives. But he could have sent flowers or a representative and considered his duty met.

Now Jackson's hazel-eyed gaze also held sympathy for Liz. "I'm sorry your first weeks in Pleasant Creek have been anything but pleasant."

"Who could have predicted this?" Liz tried to smile.

"No one." Jackson shook his head. "This kind of thing doesn't happen here."

Mary Ann lowered her voice. "You don't really think Isaac Borkholder killed Peabody, do you?"

Approaching the open grave and closed casket, Jackson murmured something Liz couldn't hear. His wrinkled forehead, though, told Liz the mayor appeared to harbor doubts too.

A larger, heavier version of Clarence wearing an outdated suit raised his eyebrows at their arrival and identified himself as Gene Peabody. Mary Ann introduced everyone to him and to sandy-haired Tom Yoder. Gene thanked them for their attendance but said little else. He completely ignored several reporters who hovered in the background. An elderly pastor read Psalm 23 and reviewed Clarence's life. Liz didn't hear anything she hadn't read in his online obituary, other than that his father had been an itinerant construction laborer during Clarence's childhood. Clarence and Gene had followed in their father's footsteps, eventually co-owning Peabody Construction in Evansville. The pastor soft-pedaled Clarence's sole ownership at the time of his death.

The split did not surprise Liz, especially if Gene possessed a similar personality. *How long ago did he leave the partnership?*

She gulped. Did a violent Cain-Abel quarrel precipitate the end to their relationship?

As the pastor spoke, Liz stole looks at Gene. His expression hardly changed throughout the service, though he frequently fidgeted with his tie.

Surely, though, he felt the sting of his brother's death, as she had experienced with the loss of her mother. Liz breathed a silent prayer for Gene, with no family or friends to support him at the funeral.

After the service, Gene again expressed appreciation for their thoughtfulness. On the outside possibility he might want company later, Liz invited him to coffee hour at the inn. Gene's terseness, however, made it clear that he did not plan to connect with anyone.

Liz wished she could remain at the cemetery. Perhaps, hidden behind a clump of pines near Clarence's grave, she could discover Gene's true emotions as he stood alone. She could have followed him and noted his movements while in Pleasant Creek.

But new guests were due to arrive around three thirty. Maybe she or Mary Ann could talk to Tom about Gene tomorrow. Liz hurriedly unlocked her car.

Oblivious, Mary Ann chatted on and on with Jackson. Finally, Liz started the car, and her friend took the hint. Once out of the cemetery, Liz's foot pushed the accelerator above the speed limit.

"I'm sorry. I didn't realize you needed to leave." Mary Ann eyed the speedometer. "The next time you're in a rush, we'll take the Sew Welcome van. The police never stop it when Sadie speeds."

Liz could believe that. Nailing Sadie for a traffic violation might prove more trouble than it was worth.

She let up, but her thoughts flew at warp speed to the inn. The Feeney-Fitzgeralds had requested that all bedding be laundered. Curtains, pillows, and rugs were to be removed because Mrs. Feeney-Fitzgerald suffered from allergies. Had Kiera, who placed fresh flowers in guest rooms, remembered to hold off?

After pulling into the garage, she and Mary Ann encountered Kiera scrubbing a big soapy lump in an old tin tub.

Oh, the indignity, said Beans's miserable face. With his fluffy bonnet of suds, he resembled a giant, hairy baby.

"Sadie said he needed a bath, but she had to wait on customers." Kiera sloshed the bulldog with a stream of water. "He's easy to wash. Hardly moves a muscle."

"Good idea." Liz had given up trying to clarify her orders from the Sew Welcome owners'. "Did you remember that the new guests can't have flowers in their room?"

Kiera nodded as she soaped up Beans again. Liz hurried inside and made a beeline for the Amish Room, dust rag in hand. Standing still, she let the sheer pleasure of its understated beauty sink in. The renovation of the room and her search for antiques had paid off. The massive walnut bed, with its simple lines, featured a benchlike love seat attached to its footboard. A quilt appliquéd with silhouettes of Amish figures and scenes against blue, gold, and dark red backgrounds covered the bed. She missed the patchwork pillows that normally livened the room and the homey rag rugs that accented the rich beauty of the polished wood floor; they had been removed as potential allergens. A bouquet of red and white roses in a blue-and-white pitcher on the dresser would have added a lovely finishing touch.

While wielding her dust rag, she found the room unbearably stuffy and almost opened the window. She'd hoped to delay using central air-conditioning. Could she afford to turn it on for only one couple?

Stop fussing and do it. Liz finished and then darted down the stairs when the chimes rang. A tall, thin woman wearing a flowing muslin dress towered over a gray-ponytailed man. Liz summoned her warmest hostess smile. "Mr. and Mrs. Feeney-Fitzgerald?"

"Yes." The woman moved past Liz, revolving slowly, hands raised. "What a lovely old home. Echoes of the past. Regeneration for the future. The energy here will suit us, don't you think, Salathiel?"

"I miss the mountains, but I already sense the strength of the land." Salathiel closed his eyes and stood stock-still.

Neither spoke.

Liz looked from one to the other. Registration might take longer than she'd expected.

Fortunately, Salathiel's eyes popped open. He signed them in while his wife continued her slow, circling meditation. Her name was Aurora-Dawn. Had her parents thought the redundancy would emphasize her ethereal qualities? No doubt, computers did interesting things to people with hyphenated first *and* last names.

When Liz advised Salathiel of the Olde Mansion's amenities, his lined face lit with a surprisingly sweet smile. "I'll bake something for coffee hour. Everyone loves my lemon-lavender bread."

"I always enjoy new recipes." Liz welcomed guest participation, but she'd also bake her usual batch because Jim Baylor would expect his beloved cookies. "Let me know what ingredients you need, Salathiel."

He nodded. "We also will search the fields for what Mother Earth provides."

His wife awakened from her trance and asked, "Did you remove the allergy-inducing elements from our room?"

Liz affirmed her precautions, though privately she wondered why her inn's room had to be allergy-free and Mother Earth's fields didn't.

"Thank you." Aurora-Dawn smiled. "Not everyone is so considerate."

The doorbell rang again. Liz excused herself to receive the UPS carrier, as Mary Ann was expecting a special shipment. The Feeney-Fitzgeralds followed to fetch their luggage.

While she signed for the package, a smelly ball of soapy twigs, grass cuttings, and trash rolled in through the open door like a toxic snowball. Kiera plunged past Liz at full speed.

"Aaaaahhhh! I'm allergic to dogs!" Aurora-Dawn wailed, holding up her skirts as if crossing a cesspool.

Beans did reek, Liz conceded. Recovering in a split second, she joined Kiera in trying to grab the slippery animal, but he escaped and shook several questionable layers onto Aurora-Dawn.

Shrieking, she sprinted out to their vintage VW bus. Salathiel, a step behind, yelled, "It's all right, babe!" and "Don't sit on the upholstery!"

Sadie charged out of Sew Welcome. "Poor Beans! What happened?"

At the sound of her voice, the bulldog dropped as if shot, a piteous whimper issuing from his suddenly slack mouth. Sadie knelt beside him.

"I'm so sorry." Tears rolled down Kiera's dirty face. "Beans sat still in the tub and looked so nice and clean. We were almost finished when he just bolted."

Assured Beans had suffered no major damage, Sadie's wrath melted away. "I'm sure you did a good job. I should have warned you. He's a very sensitive dog, and all the goings-on have been hard on him. He's not himself lately."

Yes, poor, neglected thing. He'd have to suffer through another nice, warm bath while Liz tried to placate the Feeney-Fitzgeralds and air out her foyer and rotunda.

Clasping the bulldog to her heart, Sadie hoisted herself to her feet. Kiera trailed after them out the front door.

"Sweet ba-bee," Sadie crooned. "Some weeks just push you past your limits, don't they?"

Liz surveyed the muddy, stinking mess. Through the open door, she watched the VW bus roar down the street.

Poor Beans. She held her head in her hands. *I know exactly how you feel.*

8

Balancing her coffee mug, Liz slid onto the bench in the backyard. She made honorary room for her mother, as usual, but longing for her mom's steady, gray-blue eyes, the touch of her warm hand, eclipsed Liz's pretense. *If only you could talk with me, even for a few minutes.* Maybe then, she wouldn't feel the sting of the Feeney-Fitzgeralds' phone call earlier that morning, demanding their deposit back. Hopefully, these lovers of the simple life disliked technology as much as Aurora-Dawn hated Beans. Perhaps that would prevent them from scattering scathing reviews about the Olde Mansion Inn all over the Internet.

Liz sighed. Stroking the faded yellow cover of her mom's diary made her feel worse and better at the same time. She'd allowed first work, then the past few weeks' chaos to distract her from her original purpose in coming to Pleasant Creek. Carefully, she opened fragile pages to the bookmarked December entries that chronicled her mom's first Christmas in Boston. The contrast between her Amish community's thoughtful, simple celebration and Advent in the city had flabbergasted young Abigail.

Indeed, I expect any day to encounter a neon Nativity. Has no one in this town ever seen or smelled a real barn?

It is so smoggy here. I miss the cold, pure nights in Indiana, where we could see a thousand stars and remember the Wise Men's faith in following the one Star to the Savior. Few here seem to truly worship Him.

But then, a star does not always shine so pure elsewhere either.

Liz reread the last sentence. *What did Mom mean?* It seemed a random thing to say.

She examined the diary's cover, inside and out. There were no sketches of stars. She leafed through pages she'd already read. There was not even a mention of stars.

Lying back on the bench and closing her eyes, she let her thoughts wander to conversations she and her mother had shared, especially during her illness's last stage. They'd often spoken of heaven. But Liz couldn't recall anything about stars, galaxies, the North Star, Dippers, Andromeda . . . her brain spurted stream-of-consciousness associations that soared and then faded like comet tails.

The breeze was blowing a little cool. Naomi, delivering croissants earlier that morning, had commented on the crisp day, unusual for the last part of May. Liz shivered, wishing she'd worn a jacket. Better yet, she should have brought her mom's baby quilt to drape around her shoulders.

The quilt. Liz sat up straight. Did its many-pieced single star hold some clue she'd missed? Was there a clue that might light the way to finding her relatives?

Possibly. Yet the reference didn't seem positive. How could Liz reconcile a star on the quilt that been her mother's since she was a baby with a star that adult Abigail felt "didn't always shine so pure?" Perhaps its symbolism held negative elements Liz knew nothing about. She'd ask Mary Ann or Sadie. Liz half-rose to consult one of her quilt experts that very moment and then realized if she did, the mundane duties of an innkeeper would catch her in its hamster wheel. *When will I get another chance to read Mom's diary without interruption?*

Liz dropped back onto the bench and reviewed her afternoon

schedule on her phone, surprised to find nothing until coffee hour. The Baylors had gone exploring, and she anticipated no new guests today. She'd painted and cleaned every day for weeks. Sarah was finishing trim in the second-floor Heirloom room, and Kiera doing the same in the third-floor Sunrise room. Liz hoped that having them work on separate floors would buy some momentary peace.

Given Liz's recent track record, she knew she'd better relax and read while she could. Besides, the next entries might explain her mom's cryptic star reference.

The following pages continued her mother's Christmas saga: her wonder at the lighting of a fifty-foot Christmas tree on Boston Common and the free skating extravaganza that accompanied it; her desperation to find a job, any job, with no experience and limited schooling; the absurdity of finally landing one as a reindeer at a mall and wearing antlers instead of a Kapp! Liz laughed until she nearly fell off the bench. Then tears dribbled down her cheeks at her mother's deep loneliness during her first holiday away from her family. Both laughing and crying released the tension twisted up inside her. Reading the diary didn't replace hearing her mother's husky-yet-feminine voice over the phone or seeing her in a face-to-face conversation that was almost always punctuated with warm pats and hugs. Still, it helped.

Yet her mom had not answered the question that gnawed at Liz: *Why* did Abigail leave her family?

The diary portrayed her mother's adventurous spirit, her resourcefulness, and her openness to new experiences. So far, Liz hadn't noticed any anger toward Abigail's parents, or rebellion toward their religion or way of life.

She read and pondered until her phone's *ding* reminded her to bake cookies for coffee hour. She rose, dashed down to the shoreline, and skipped two stones—an art her mother had taught her during summer camping trips. The rocks joyfully skittered across the water's wavy surface and then dropped with satisfying *plunks*.

Picking up the diary and her coffee mug, she returned to the inn, baked phenomenal fudge-nut bars, and shared a pleasant coffee hour with her guests.

"What a sweet quilt!" Mary Ann, standing behind her shop's old-fashioned glass notion case, caressed the blue, yellow, and creamy folds of the baby quilt with loving fingers. "The prints are unique, yet complement each other so well. Look at that stitching!"

"Such a lovely *Steppdecke*!" two Amish customers exclaimed while they examined the quilt's workmanship.

Why this small surge of family pride? Liz didn't even know if a family member had made it.

"The hand stitching is so perfect, it almost looks as if a machine sewed it," said Caitlyn, who had dropped in and was squinting at the stitches. "Do you think I'll ever get that good?"

"You're better now than I was at your age," Sadie assured her.

Since her irrational explosion about Emily, Sadie had cooled down, as Mary Ann had predicted. Now her sparkly blue eyes scanned Liz's quilt. "Did your grandma make it? Or did you find it at a flea market?"

"My mother gave it to me." Liz hoped no one would notice the small E.H. stitched near one corner. Could she manage to keep her family quest private awhile longer?

"Star of Bethlehem." Mary Ann smoothed a wrinkle. "It's a classic Amish pattern, though not usually used for baby quilts. You might consider displaying it in the rotunda on a rack—you know, in that bare spot. It would add such a lovely touch."

"You're right." *As usual.* Liz would shop for a rack that week, though she'd borrow her quilt when she needed a good snuggle.

Sadie, Caitlyn, and the customers wandered off to look at newly arrived fabrics. Liz wanted to keep the Star of Bethlehem discussion going. Trying to keep her tone casual, she said, "Does it symbolize anything other than the Christmas star? Anything sad or difficult?"

Mary Ann's glance felt like the first touch of a dentist's probe. "Not that I know of."

Liz thought maybe she'd better change the subject after all. She lowered her volume from a "chat" to a "confide" level. "I meant to ask you if you could talk to your funeral director friend about Gene Peabody."

Mary Ann pursed her lips. "You wonder if he killed Clarence."

Liz blinked. "He left the partnership, and he didn't exactly seem destroyed by Clarence's death."

"That would make perfect sense," Mary Ann agreed, "except that Tom told me the police had to track down Gene in Arizona to notify him about Clarence. He lives in Lafayette but was attending a construction convention in Phoenix at the time of the murder."

"So much for my Cain-Abel theory." Liz grimaced. "It fit so well—"

"Miss Eckardt?"

Liz started. Sarah had materialized in Sew Welcome, silent as a grave. She looked like an angel statue in a cemetery—stiff with a gray complexion, but with dark circles under her eyes. Liz asked, "Is something wrong?"

"I haven't finished the painting." The girl chiseled her words as if out of granite. "But I'll do it early tomorrow, if you don't mind."

If you don't mind? Sarah's tone said, "Take it or leave it."

The Material Girls and the customers blinked in unison. One Amish lady's eyebrows disappeared into her hair.

"That will be fine." Liz's arm encircled the girl's rigid shoulders and gently steered her out of the shop to her own quarters.

Kiera peered down from the stairs, grinning like a gargoyle.

Apparently, a flight of stairs between the two hadn't been enough distance. At the moment, even a light-year might not suffice.

Nevertheless, Liz opened her door and beckoned. "Kiera, please join us for iced tea."

"I will not sit with her." Sarah crossed her arms.

"Fine." Kiera flounced past them. "I wouldn't sit by you if you paid me a million dollars."

Great. Liz edged Sarah into the room. She remained standing. Kiera dropped onto the sofa. Liz said, "Let's just take a few deep breaths, okay?"

Both scowled. Liz turned away, pouring tea as if they'd agreed.

Liz handed the tumblers to the teens. "I don't know why you're fighting, but you're both intelligent young women. Surely, you can work this out—"

"She'll say I took the best paintbrush," Kiera fumed, "but she used it yesterday."

"At least I clean it the right way. You've left a mess in the garage. Paint all over the sink. All over the floor." Sarah's righteous tone sliced like a paper cut. She set her untasted tea on the coffee table. "I am glad to do my share and more, Miss Eckardt, but I do not consider cleaning up after *her* my job."

Kiera sat up straight. "I always clean up after I'm done. I just don't follow *your* schedule."

Liz tried to interrupt. "We all do things differently—"

"Miss Perfect may fuss about how I paint, but that's not why she hates me." Kiera's feline eyes narrowed. "She wanted me to lie to the police about Mr. Peabody's being into her."

Fire flashed from Sarah's eyes, so searing that Liz stepped between them.

"Isaac wouldn't be in jail if it weren't for you!" Sarah cried.

She fled the room and the inn, leaving Kiera calmly drinking her tea and Liz wondering if she should have bought a bed-and-breakfast in a more peaceful place—say, the Middle East.

"I didn't realize how little attention I paid to the road until I moved here." Riding in the Sew Welcome van, Liz watched Mary Ann brake for yet another Amish buggy.

"You've had a lot to think about." Mary Ann waved at the driver, a woman with children, whose bonnets and straw hats bobbed behind her. "Watching for buggies will become second nature before you know it." Mary Ann turned onto a gravel road and then into a long lane. "This is the Yoder farm."

Did messy animals really live in that pristine white barn? Liz glanced at her denim skirt. She'd changed from jeans, anxious not to offend the Yoders.

Mary Ann seemed to read her mind. "The Amish don't expect others to keep their rules. They only ask to be allowed to follow their way of life."

"Good." Liz leaned her head on her hand. "I'm not sure what to say."

"You won't have to say much." Mary Ann slowed at the sight of an oncoming wagon. "That you came will show that you care."

Liz hoped so. She did care about Sarah, her devastation at Isaac's situation, and her need for income. Liz also cared about her inn. The last-minute cancellations she'd feared because of the murder had not occurred. Three rooms would be filled this weekend.

Mary Ann pulled into a driveway beside a plain white house with eye-popping flower gardens. Such a kaleidoscope of color!

Yet the Amish man who appeared on the front porch wore the typical near-colorless uniform: black pants, blue shirt with no buttons, and wide-brimmed hat. His familiar round sun-browned face, blond hair, and keen eyes more than hinted that he was Sarah's father.

Mary Ann exited the driver's seat. "Evening, Jeremiah."

"Evening." The farmer cocked his head at Liz but said nothing.

Mary Ann gestured. "This is Liz Eckardt, Sarah's boss."

He nodded. And still said nothing.

"I'm pleased to meet you," Liz said.

Mary Ann had told her she wouldn't have to say much, but it seemed Liz would have to carry the whole conversation. "May I speak with Sarah, please?"

Mary Ann squeezed her hand and returned to the van. Jeremiah opened the screen door. Without raising his voice, he called his daughter. Sarah walked through the door like a marionette, with a wooden face to match.

"I appreciate your work very much, Sarah," Liz said.

"Thank you."

Silence.

Liz tried again. "I'm sure we can work things out between you and Kiera. But for now, she will do outside work only."

The girl's stiff shoulders relaxed slightly. "That would be . . . better."

Liz did not detect any movement from Jeremiah, but at some signal from him, Sarah continued, "I-I'm sorry I ran away. I did mean to return."

Relief gushed through Liz. "I'm sorry you're going through such difficult time right now. I didn't mean to add to it." Actually, she'd tried to lighten Sarah's load by assigning some indoor work to Kiera.

With her hand, Sarah tried to capture a rebel tear. "If things were . . . normal, I don't think I would have reacted the way I did."

"Hard times affect all of us." Liz continued the "we're talking about Isaac but we won't mention his name" conversation for a moment longer. At the end of their talk, she patted the girl's shoulder.

"I will bring her over early tomorrow to paint," Jeremiah said.

Liz thanked them both again. To her surprise, Sarah gave her a quick hug.

Liz exhaled as she returned to the van. She'd done the right thing—this time. Flopping into the passenger seat, she realized the short conversation had drained her.

"Good job." Mary Ann warmed her with an approving smile.

"I have so much to learn about the Amish." Liz drank in the delicious fragrance of freshly cut hay blowing through the open window. "I hope I understand their ways before—"

Before I meet my family. She'd almost said it.

Fortunately, another buggy had turned into the lane, distracting Mary Ann from noticing.

Liz hoped.

9

"I know what we need around here." Pinning patterns to fabric, Sadie spoke through a half-dozen straight pins tucked in her mouth. As usual, she made herself perfectly clear. "We need a birthday party."

"Yaayyy!" The word "party" infused life into a quilting session that, by Material Girls' standards, had matched the grayness of the stormy evening outside.

Liz stopped cutting red diamond shapes for a Christmas project and laid aside her shears. "Good idea."

Thankfully, Liz and Mary Ann had managed to keep Emily and Sadie apart until the librarian left. But the murder and Isaac's incarceration continued to shroud each day. What with Sarah and Kiera's quarrel and still shaky cease-fire, plus the departure of the sunshiny Baylors and the other guests on Sunday, they all needed a lift. But . . .

"Do you know anyone who's actually having a birthday?" Liz asked, hoping Sadie hadn't planned to simply grab a guest of honor off the street.

"Of course I do." Sadie lifted her chin. "Beans."

"Beans?" Liz's prior experience with pets was very limited. She'd had two goldfish named Barbie and Ken. She hadn't thrown birthday parties for them. *Was I a deadbeat fish mom?*

Caitlyn clapped her hands. "I'll bring the cakes."

"Fabulous plan," Sadie said.

"Cakes?" Liz sputtered. Just how many people would be invited to her inn?

"Caitlyn makes the best butter cake you ever tasted." Mary Ann high-fived Caitlyn, who beamed.

For once, Opal seemed in full agreement with Sadie. "My cousin

Faye's cakes used to win grand-champion ribbons at the fair every year. But Caitlyn's have topped Faye's the last two years."

"Um, when is this birthday party taking place?" Liz changed the subject before the two could further discuss fairs and champion ribbons.

"On Beans's birthday, of course." Sadie wrinkled her nose. "The twenty-eighth of May. Thursday afternoon."

Two days from now. Hopefully, lack of time would prevent this celebration from growing into a county-wide event.

"Are you sure he'll be awake?" Liz asked. Beans not only took frequent naps, he cherished his early-to-bed beauty sleep.

Sadie sniffed. "No one has ever slept through a birthday party I've thrown."

"That's the truth." Naomi waggled her eyebrows at Liz.

Sadie swayed her blue-jeaned rear in an impromptu dance. "We'll keep those puppies movin' and groovin' till midnight."

Puppies? Liz knew she shouldn't be surprised, but . . . how many dogs? *Till midnight?*

"Don't let her scare you," Mary Ann whispered as Sadie and Caitlyn joined in one of their weird and wonderful tangos. "I'll rein her in. Besides, we'll have the party outside."

Liz began to breathe again.

"Unless it rains."

On the day of Beans's party, the sky experimented with ten different shades of gray, ranging from almost blue to menacing charcoal, keeping Liz on the edge of her seat. Undaunted, six canine birthday guests showed up, accompanied by young relatives of the Material Girls, each with an adult relative. Liz, praying fervently for any reason to cancel the party, hadn't considered the fun of children and dogs frolicking in her backyard. Nor had she anticipated the positive PR the bash was generating with adults. They marveled at the paw-print banners and streamers, and the colorful paper Japanese lanterns the Material Girls had hung in the gazebo. "Thanks for doing this for our kids—and our dogs!"

Along with his favorite rug, Sadie hauled Beans to the backyard. He sniffed his approval of the other doggy smells and even raised his head once. His gaudy jeweled birthday crown slid sideways and caught on one ear. Sadie left it that way. "It gives him a debonair look, don't you think?"

Elmo, an Irish setter, escaped his leash, resulting in a universal race to capture him. Caitlyn and her nephew managed to grab Elmo before he jumped into the lake. Freddy, a darling basset hound puppy that kept tripping over his long ears, ate his party hat but appeared to suffer no ill effects. All in all, the canine guests seemed well-behaved. Liz even said as much.

Sadie acted insulted. "You think I would invite doggy delinquents?"

Naomi saved Liz the trouble of replying by shooing everyone toward a mini obstacle course Opal's husband, George, had set up. The canines accomplished near-Olympic feats—at least, in their young handlers' opinions. The biggest applause, however, erupted when Caitlyn and Naomi carried cakes out of the inn, candles ablaze. For the human guests, Caitlyn had sculpted a magnificent brown-and-white bust of Beans.

Given the bulldog's perpetual immobility, it was tough to tell the two apart, flickering candles aside.

Beans didn't seem particularly impressed at first. But with a whiff of the second cake, he sat up.

Intrigued, Liz followed his gaze—and the other dogs'—to the large round cake Naomi carried, its sides swathed in bacon, its top a pinwheel of bologna slices.

"Bologna's his favorite!" Sadie clasped her hands as several pups tugged at their leashes. "What's inside?"

"Meat loaf." Naomi gestured to the children. "These dogs won't wait long. Let's hurry and sing *Happy Birthday*. Then Beans will need help blowing out the candles."

He attacked his mammoth piece of birthday cake with all the energy he'd saved up during the past year and then licked his chops with the biggest doggy smile Liz had seen.

"His can't possibly be as good as yours," she told Caitlyn. "This cake is to die for!"

The Material Girls all looked at her.

What unfortunate wording. Liz closed her eyes. She'd almost forgotten about the murder. Now she'd managed to remind everyone else about it too.

"Who wants to see Buster dance?" Sadie whistled for her grandson Sam's fox terrier and turned up her phone. As strains of *Who Let the Dogs Out* serenaded the party, Buster pranced on his hind legs, imitating Sadie's and Sam's moves. Caitlyn's rescued greyhound, Kelly, stretched her long, slim body, partnering with her mistress. Beans wagged his tail three times. The children laughed and danced with them.

This party really might go on until midnight. Liz threw her friends grateful looks. *I hope it does.*

But the weather had other ideas. Thunder growled and then crashed, and a bolt of lightning streaked across the sky. Everyone grabbed children, dogs, and the remaining food, and dashed to the back porch.

Elmo slipped off his leash again and raced past Liz through the open back door and into the inn, generating a chase that required most of the adults to catch him.

Finally successful, the adult chaperones took advantage of a lull in the falling rain and herded their children and dogs into cars. A chorus of goodbyes and well wishes warmed Liz's heart.

Beans had lost his birthday crown. He sprawled on his rug as if boneless.

"Too much party, old boy?" Liz patted his head, then gestured to the Material Girls. "We'll let him sleep it off, but is anybody else up for coffee?"

"Yes!" Opal cast her vote. "Let's finish off the birthday cake."

"You can eat meat loaf." Sadie elbowed her away from it. "I need sugar."

Flopped on a living room settee, Liz smiled as the group, similarly flopped, bantered and laughed.

Who would have thought that a dog party could be so fun? And so healing?

Her euphoria, however, did not last long.

Mary Ann's keen glance touched the childhood picture of Liz's mother on the mantel. "What a lovely photo." Mary Ann swiveled her gaze to Liz, waiting for her to identify it.

"Thanks." Liz sidestepped her. "I like how it looks with that teacup and lavender arrangement."

"They do look nice together." Mary Ann cocked her head. "That young woman reminds me of someone I worked with years ago in my family's fabric shop—long before we called it Sew Welcome."

"Hmm. Ooh, it looks like you all could use some more coffee." Liz escaped to the kitchen, took a deep breath, and busied herself making a fresh pot.

As soon as everyone left, she removed her mother's photo from the mantel and placed it in her private sitting room, away from prying eyes.

10

Matching her full coffee mug, Liz's Sunday brimmed with warmth and anticipation. She always looked forward to attending Pleasant Creek Community Church, whose friendly membership included all the Material Girls. Plus, later that afternoon, she would get to talk to her godson, Steve!

Sadie, sporting a spectacular hat that seemed to fill her shocking pink Jeep, picked up Liz.

"Cute dress." Sadie eyed Liz's black cotton sheath. "But it needs something. Maybe a hat."

Liz quickly steered Sadie away from fashion advice by asking about her grandson. In no time, they were pulling into the church parking lot.

Sometimes Liz missed her large Boston church, with its modern worship service and high-tech gadgets, but she appreciated the closeness of her new one too. Pastor Brad's sermon about Jesus's command to love one's neighbor probed her heart. Thoughts of Miriam Borkholder took root as the congregation sang the doxology. How was Miriam handling the strain of her son's incarceration? Would she welcome a visit or regard it as invasive? *After all, you've only seen Miriam a few times at Sew Welcome.*

After the benediction, Liz trailed after Sadie, who chatted with everyone.

"Have things settled down at the inn?" Jackson Cross's voice tugged at her.

She summoned a smile. "Somewhat."

Sadie broke in. "Jackie, you missed the best birthday bash of the year."

"Birthday bash? When? Whose?"

"Last Thursday Beans turned seven!" Sadie clucked at him. "I called you to come over and party, but you never got back to me."

"I'm sorry. I was in Chicago."

Jackson sounded genuinely disappointed. But his glance detoured toward Liz. Unless she was badly mistaken, the mayor's thoughts weren't centered on Beans. Keeping her smile intact, Liz fidgeted inwardly. *Please. No guests are due today. I only want Steve's call, a good book, and a nap. And maybe a visit to Miriam's.*

Fortunately, Sadie's everlasting descriptions of Beans's cakes, the decorations, the doggy guests, and their escapades sufficiently dulled the gleam in Jackson's eyes. Liz found herself being driven safely away in Sadie's Jeep, waving goodbye to the mayor, who looked a little dazed.

Sadie zoomed down the road, almost running one of the few stoplights. She tapped on the wheel impatiently and then said, "Aren't you going to thank me?"

Liz almost said, "For what?" But her friend's broad grin stopped her. Liz gasped. "Did you deliberately stonewall Jackson?"

"Jackson? Are you talking about some general?" Sadie's innocent eyes under the brim of the big hat disappeared with her face-crinkling, wicked laugh.

"Sadie Schwarzentruber." Liz giggled with her. *The Crazy Quilter strikes again.*

"I knew you didn't want him to ask you out. Though I can't imagine why not." Sadie hit the accelerator. "Jackson is a smart, kind, Christian man. Plus, he's got *lovely* muscles."

Liz, who'd been thinking the same thing, flushed. "He is nice. I'm sure he's an excellent mayor. But I don't need extra complications right now."

"You're so right, dear." Sadie patted her on the arm. "You've had a rough start in Pleasant Creek. Give yourself some breathing room."

Liz took Sadie's advice, even to the point of refusing a fried-chicken-dinner invitation from Sadie herself. Instead, she took a sandwich and a best-selling thriller outside to her favorite bench just as her phone *dinged.*

A text from Steve! Her godson had arrived safely at his base. She urged him to eat something—he had a habit of skipping meals—and then call her.

A few lilac blossoms still lingered, scenting the air. The sun dappled the lake with sparkles, and a drowsy breeze played with her hair. But Steve's text had chased away any thoughts of a nap, especially as she pondered how to tell him that her new, peaceful life had been blitzed by a murder. Liz sighed, saying a quick prayer of thanks that her godson had returned from his mission, safe and sound. She couldn't wait to hear his voice.

Her phone rang. *He always was a fast eater.* "Steve?"

"Mom."

It was only one word, but it gave her a head-to-toe smile. He couldn't relate much about his mission, but he told her about his friends, including a younger, homesick soldier he'd taken under his wing. Liz described the Material Girls and a serene version of Pleasant Creek, deciding it best not to cause him any worry on her account.

Finally, Steve said, "I checked out the *Pleasant Creek Tribune* online while I ate. I thought I might see something about the inn but not about a murder. Are you sure you're safe there?"

Blasted Internet. "I'm fine," she said firmly. "The mayor told me this never happens here, so I don't expect a repeat for at least a hundred years. Besides, my friends take good care of me." She described how Sadie, Mary Ann, and Beans had dispatched Matt, and Steve roared with laughter.

When he could speak again, he said, "I never did like that guy. Sounds like you're in good hands. But I wish I could be there too."

"Maybe you can visit at Christmas?" Liz steered him toward thoughts of the holidays. She even weaseled out of promising to call him if anything else happened. *Son, we both know you can't come.*

After they hung up, she decided she couldn't relax so close to the place where Peabody died and ventured inside. Yet the house seemed so empty and . . . lonely. *When was the last time I was the only person here?* Her footsteps echoed in the kitchen as she grabbed a container of yogurt from the fridge.

She could hardly endure thoughts of the dangers Steve faced. But did Miriam, agonizing over her son in jail, feel even more alone than Liz?

After finishing her snack, Liz retrieved Miriam's address from her property tax records. She couldn't call beforehand. Even if the Borkholders owned a phone, she was sure they wouldn't answer it on Sunday. She checked her smartphone GPS for the easiest route to the out-in-the-boonies farm.

Then she glanced at the clock. She didn't want to intrude on Miriam's family's evening meal. More waiting. Liz stripped beds and tossed sheets and pillowcases into the heavy-duty washer she'd splurged on. At six o'clock, she jumped into her car and headed out of town.

Thousands of young corn plants waved friendly leaves at her as she drove. Cows switched lazy tails in pastures sprinkled with daisies and purple clover.

If only the pictures in her mind matched the tranquil countryside. Instead she saw a man murdered . . . Miriam's heartbroken days . . . Sarah's white, angry face . . . *What can I do, God, to help my neighbors?*

Despite her difficult start as an innkeeper, Liz had no intention of practicing law again—certainly not criminal law. But perhaps she could steer Miriam and her husband, Philip, toward someone who could help with their son's defense.

She couldn't have imagined a flower garden prettier than the Yoders', but a rainbow of color greeted Liz as she pulled into the Borkholders' gravel driveway. Throwing open her car door, she sat for a moment, inhaling the scent. Pink, red, yellow, coral, and lavender roses all poured out their beauty and fragrance for the world to enjoy.

"Liz?" Miriam stood on the front porch, looking as if she couldn't quite believe her eyes.

Liz walked toward her. She extended a hand, almost at the same time Miriam reached for hers.

Liz said, "I hope I'm not interrupting your family time."

"We visited with our families earlier. Philip is resting, the older children left for the Sunday night singing, and the girls are taking a walk." A tiny smile tried to hide the slight trembling of Miriam's lips but didn't quite succeed. "It is a good time to sit on the porch. Would you like coffee? Water?"

"Water would be nice."

Sitting in the rockers on the big white house's front porch, Liz wished they could share a contented silence or speak of recipes or quilting patterns. But Miriam's pain colored the air, as sure as the roses did the view. "Is there any way I can help you? I'm not licensed to practice law in Indiana, but I could find someone who could—"

"We will not consult a lawyer. That is not our way." Though another tear trickled down Miriam's face, her quiet words matched the iron set of her jaw. "Isaac is in the hands of Gött."

Miriam's attitude disturbed Liz, but she wasn't surprised. "How is Isaac?"

Her friend's glance darted toward the front door. Bowing her head, she murmured, "Mary Ann says he is well."

"You haven't seen him?"

Miriam raised her head like a doe sniffing danger. Then, a tear creeping from one eye, she whispered, "He has committed *der Mord*. We must shun him."

Even as a child, Liz had not been given to tantrums, but she wanted to throw one now. *How can you do this?* she longed to yell. *Families do not leave their children alone when they are in need!* If Steve ever found himself in trouble, she would fight to the death to defend him.

But I'm not Miriam. And I'm not Amish. Liz knew she shouldn't make snap judgments. Criticizing her friend's convictions would only add to Miriam's pain and slam the door on their blossoming friendship.

So she did what she thought would help Miriam the most. She prayed silently for God's mercy. For Miriam. For Isaac. For Sarah.

Until little Keturah skipped in from the barn, she and Miriam simply sat, clinging to each other's hands, drinking in the sweet splendor of the roses. Right then, it seemed enough.

The next afternoon, Liz carved out a couple of hours to research at Pleasant Creek's stately old library. The librarian assisted her in learning how to operate the ancient microfiche reader, and Liz scanned local newspapers that had been published around the time her mother left Pleasant Creek. She found three short articles about runaway Amish girls—Anna Schrock, Deborah Miller, and Martha Zook—whose separate departures all occurred during the autumn her mother left. She'd considered the unlikely possibility that her mom had changed her name, but nothing Liz found indicated any connection between these girls and her mother.

Liz's mind wandered to her mother's reference to the star that didn't shine so pure. Did her mother refer to the large, colorful stars painted on some Amish barns? She'd noticed several since moving to Pleasant Creek. Did those conceal some secret meaning? A few online articles and two library books assured her they were merely decorative, but Liz resolved to ask Miriam the next time she saw her—if her husband allowed them to meet again. Philip, upon encountering them sitting together on the porch, had remained civil, but looked none too pleased.

"He is trying to protect me," Miriam had whispered as she walked Liz to her car. "Reporters have badgered us continually."

"I understand," Liz had said. "I'll see you soon at Sew Welcome."

Though she longed to spend more time with Miriam, Liz had decided, for the time being, not to press the issue. As for the barn stars, perhaps if Sarah mellowed a bit, she might ask her about their meaning.

Liz walked home from the library, rejoicing once more that she hadn't experienced a traffic jam in weeks. True, summer had begun to heat the blacktop so it gave off its tarry smell, but sprawling buildings and skyscrapers didn't block the breezes, as they did in the city. After letting the back screen door slam behind her—she loved that sound!—Liz headed for the fridge and gulped down a glass of iced tea. Though no guests awaited coffee hour, she made peanut butter cookies and carried a plateful to Sew Welcome.

"You saved my life." Sadie threw her hand to head with a gesture of nineteenth-century melodrama. "Mary Ann didn't bring anything to eat today."

"You know I spent last evening helping my grandkids with their 4-H cooking projects," Mary Ann retorted, reaching for a cookie. "They wolfed down every last crumb. Plus, I wanted to make food for the Bontrager barn raising."

Sadie offered cookies to a customer and then wandered with her to look at quilt patterns.

Mary Ann turned her penetrating gaze on Liz. "I heard you visited Miriam yesterday."

Nothing, but nothing in Pleasant Creek escaped Mary Ann's radar.

Liz nodded. "She told me you've seen Isaac."

"Chief Houghton let me visit him the day after he was jailed, since his family can't come." Mary Ann shook her head. "I cannot believe that boy is a murderer."

Liz ventured, "Do . . . do you think Isaac might talk to me? I can't defend him, but we might discover something that could help him."

"I'd thought of that." Mary Ann's fingers arranged straight pins on a fat tomato-shaped pincushion. "Could you go with me tomorrow afternoon, if the chief approves?"

"Sure." Liz lowered her voice further. "Do you know if Sarah has visited Isaac?"

"I'm sure she hasn't." Mary Ann matched Liz's tone. "Even if she decided to throw out her own convictions, her father is probably keeping an eagle eye on her. Also, Chief Houghton would never cross Jeremiah's wishes regarding his daughter unless it meant breaking the law. The chief respects Amish ways. That's why he and the Amish community cooperate so well."

Houghton did permit them access to Isaac the next day. Liz couldn't help wincing as she and Mary Ann were searched by a policewoman and steel doors locked behind them. They entered a dingy, windowless room and sat on metal folding chairs facing a bulletproof glass window. A tall, muscular young man entered from another steel door, followed by a guard, and sat on the other side of the window. His high cheekbones, full mouth, and coloring mirrored his mother's.

His Amish haircut clashed ridiculously with the neon orange jumpsuit he wore. He'd forgotten to secure some buttons—but then, perhaps he had not forgotten at all. Though forced to wear prison clothing, perhaps Isaac was raising his small flag of defiance in the only way he could.

His indigo eyes did not look defiant. They looked haunted.

Liz had to turn her own gaze elsewhere.

"Thanks for coming," Isaac said stiffly, as if prompted by his mother.

"We've been praying for you every day, dear." Mary Ann patted the glass gently. She introduced Liz. "This lady may be able to help you, Isaac. Would you tell her your story?"

"I already talked to the police," Isaac said woodenly.

"Yes, but Ms. Eckardt would like to hear the details of what happened that day."

The young man obediently began his account. He sounded, Liz thought, like a recording. Isaac had finished his farm chores and told his parents he'd eat dinner at a friend's, where he was going to help build a shed. Instead, he'd tied his horse downtown and walked to the lake to wait for Sarah, who had agreed to meet him there after work. Having gotten off work early because she was sick, Sarah was already waiting for him. But she had grown worse and decided to catch a ride home with her neighbor instead of going out with Isaac.

Not surprisingly, Sarah hadn't mentioned that detail to Liz. Had she told Houghton? Liz prodded, "What time did she leave to meet her neighbor?"

"I don't wear a watch. But like I told Mr. Houghton, it probably was around three-thirty."

Liz, who hadn't even considered her employee as a suspect, tried to push away new doubts. Isaac had just asserted that Sarah didn't linger long at the lake. Had Chief Houghton confirmed that with the neighbor? She forced her thoughts back to the task at hand. "What did you do after that?"

"I just sat and skipped stones awhile. Then I walked around the shore opposite the inn, and around the north end. That's when I saw him."

Flames suddenly shot from Isaac's eyes.

Don't look like that, son. Liz could hardly keep her composure. "Whom did you see?"

"Clarence Peabody." Isaac's toneless monologue only made his fury more deadly. "Maybe he was hoping to meet Sarah too. Not that she wanted to see him."

"What happened?"

"We argued. He said he wouldn't stay away from her. I was afraid he would hurt my Sarah." His tanned, sinewy fists clenched.

Liz wanted to close her eyes and shut out the unsettling image of the nice young man who was painting such a dark picture. She forced herself to say it: "So you stabbed him?"

Isaac fired one raging, hopeless look at Liz and then dropped his gaze to the floor.

She tried to steady her voice. "How is it you happened to have your awl with you?"

He answered wearily, "I wore my tool belt so that when I left, my parents would not question my departure."

Of course. He'd said he was going to help build a shed. Unfortunately, the awl as Isaac's weapon did make sense now.

"Two minutes," said the guard.

Liz had forgotten the man was present. "Isaac, is there anything you want me to tell your mother?"

A spasm of pain crossed the boy's face. "Give her my love. But don't let her send for the bishop. I'm not sorry the man is dead, and Gött knows that."

11

After the jail visit, both Liz and Mary Ann agreed a very strong cup of coffee was in order.

"Actually," Mary Ann said, "I might guzzle a whole pot if Naomi's air-conditioning is going full blast."

"We need major sugar too." The minute Liz heard the bells jingle over Sweet Everything's door, she knew they'd come to the right place. The bakery's white tables and chairs set against soft gray walls exerted both a crisp and soothing effect. Coral-print paper place mats and carnations in bud vases added a pop of color. Naomi, wearing a matching coral apron, had just brewed a pot of extra-strong coffee, as she often did to help downtown coffee breakers last till five. Gratefully, Liz and Mary Ann sipped big mugfuls and nibbled a huge cupcake apiece—Liz, a cream-filled key lime one, and Mary Ann, a German chocolate one that was weighed down with pecans.

"Maybe we can make some sense of it all now." Mary Ann wiped her mouth daintily after several large bites. Naomi brought a full carafe and her own mug. She sat beside Liz.

"Aren't you going to eat?" Liz asked, still nibbling. "If I owned a bakery—"

"Exactly." Naomi grinned. "At one time, I weighed 263 pounds. Not good. Plus, I realized I shouldn't eat up all the profits." She patted Mary Ann's hand. "You two, however, looked like you needed a jump start when you came in. What's up?"

Lowering their voices, Liz and Mary Ann told her about their visit with Isaac.

Naomi whistled softly. "No wonder. I can't imagine how his family must feel. How Sarah feels."

"If only I could offer something to help him." *Forget sipping.* Liz swilled her coffee and poured herself another.

"He told you exactly the same awful story he told me right after Peabody's death." Mary Ann grimaced. "And, according to Chief Houghton, the same one he told the police."

"Exactly?" Liz frowned. "That's unusual. Most of us, when describing an event, vary the explanation a little. Come to think of it, Isaac did seem as if he were reciting something he'd memorized." She drummed her fingers on the table. "My lawyer's gut says he's innocent."

"You think so?" Naomi clasped her hands. "I hope you're right. I simply refuse to believe that nice young man would do something so awful."

"He's not telling us something, though," Liz said. "Could Isaac be protecting someone else—the person who killed Peabody?"

"Who could that be?" Naomi's eyebrows rose. "Sarah's not a suspect, is she?"

"Thankfully, no." Liz shook her head. "I spoke briefly with Houghton afterward. He confirmed with Sarah's neighbor and family that she arrived home well before five, the approximate time of the murder."

"Who else might Isaac protect?" Naomi warmed Mary Ann's coffee.

"I wish I knew," Liz said as they all exchanged blank stares.

"Clarence Peabody seemed angry at the whole Amish community." Mary Ann stirred in cream and her usual three teaspoons of sugar.

"Sarah told me that on the day Peabody died, he even blasted the bishop, saying they'd caused his bankruptcy." Liz rested her head on her hands. "Did Peabody have a real reason to target a whole group of people?"

"I'm not sure. I wonder if he used Amish workers from Pleasant Creek," Mary Ann mused. "Construction companies recruit our guys because they're such great craftsmen and they work hard."

Liz hadn't realized that. *What else am I, the new girl in town, missing?*

"I wish I knew more about his company's problems." Liz tapped her phone and pointed. "Peabody Construction's website is still up, but, of course, it says nothing about bankruptcy. The federal government posts those records online, but I'd have to know his Social Security number to access them."

Mary Ann pushed back her plate. "I imagine," she said, "that I could find that information for you. It may take a phone call or two."

Within the hour, Opal Ringenberg's nephew, a policeman in Fort Wayne, supplied the number from his department's database.

That evening, Liz conducted her own research. *Whoa. No wonder Peabody had been so upset.* His debts ran into hundreds of thousands of dollars. She also found that one of his more recent projects, a housing division called Countryside Commons, was located an hour and a half from Pleasant Creek. The homes' median selling price, though low by Boston standards, equaled luxury-home prices in Indiana. He should have made plenty of money.

Had this subdivision somehow dealt the fatal blow to Clarence Peabody's business? Were Pleasant Creek Amish workers involved? When Peabody came to town, seeking justice, who had decided he had to die, and why?

Liz searched and probed far into the night. Finally, she wrapped her aching shoulders in her mother's quilt and flopped onto her bed, only to stare at the ceiling.

Questions lurked in the darkness. Eventually, Liz came up with a plan. Mary Ann had invited her to the Bontrager barn raising. She might learn something there about the Amish construction community in Pleasant Creek. She might even inveigle a little information about Countryside Commons.

If there was a connection.

Only then did her muscles relax. Liz fell into a restless slumber teeming with stylish mansions, Amish rose gardens, and blond boys with lost, haunted eyes, bloodstains on their hands.

When her alarm sounded early the next morning, Liz's body staged a lie-in protest. Nevertheless, she prodded it out of bed. What did an average-ish cook bring to an Amish barn raising? How long should an outsider stay? She had no idea, but she'd stick close to Mary Ann, whose un-Amish heart seemed to share their rhythm. Ignoring her to-do list for the wedding guests due tomorrow, she baked her mother's delicious recipe for macaroni and cheese with ham. Fresh fruit salad and two emergency loaves of orange-nut bread from the freezer completed her contribution. Would they suffice?

She changed to her denim skirt, loaded the food into her Acura, and tried to remember Mary Ann's directions. Though her friend had grown up in Pleasant Creek, she didn't seem to know street names and scorned addresses as irrelevant. Liz passed the lumberyard, so she was on the right track. Next she was supposed to turn right at the old Schwartz place. Was this *Haunted House* movie lookalike Mary Ann's landmark?

The unswerving routes of two wagons and a buggy slowed her progress but assured her she was going the right way. She parked in a field among rows upon rows of Amish vehicles. Anticipating a second trip back to her car, she carried her casserole toward the typical big, white house. Already, partial walls of wooden studs rose from a nearby cement-block foundation. Lines of young men and older boys methodically fed boards to those who measured and nailed so quickly the walls seemed to grow each time Liz blinked. She wondered if the men's full beards bothered them, working on warm June days like this one.

Tables under shady sycamores held jugs and snacks. A few groups of Amish women, spring pastel dresses fresh and uniform as their flower borders, clustered near the barn. Most wore the black Kapp that identified them as married. A few stared at Liz. A few smiled. Most continued their conversation in "Swiss," the local German dialect.

Her feet wanted to turn back toward her car, but Liz aimed her steps toward the house. She came to a dead stop, however, when a chorus of yodeling drifted from the screen door and open windows. She'd heard it in brief snatches on country radio stations but never in harmonies like these.

Mary Ann waved from the porch's back door. "There you are," she said. "Ooh, that looks wonderful."

She introduced Liz to Loretta Bontrager, the hostess, who welcomed the casserole with thanks and a pleasant but uncertain smile. Several women sitting on porch swings and straight wooden chairs nodded, their hands busy with mending and crocheting.

The minute Liz and Mary Ann entered, the yodeling stopped as if someone had thrown a switch. The large, steamy kitchen bloomed with Amish women of all ages, chopping, stirring, and slicing. Various kettles bubbled on the immense woodstove, sending out clouds of fragrances that blended into one big "mmm." Though Mary Ann had assured Liz that they all spoke English, the cooks, too, used the Swiss dialect. Like the men raising the barn, they all fit together like a living quilt, bonded to each other in warmth and artistry.

Could she even begin to belong here? Liz spoke up, "Is Miriam Borkholder here today? I haven't seen her."

The women raised a wall of silence.

Even as heat crept up Liz's neck, she understood they meant no hostility. Yet she wished she was in Boston. Or maybe Japan . . .

"Miriam's feeling poorly," Loretta said.

Liz thought she'd better leave before her mouth sank her in this sea of awkwardness. "I, uh, need to return to my car for the other food I brought."

"My Leah can help you." Loretta barely gestured toward a pigtailed girl who accompanied Liz out the door, Mary Ann trailing in their wake. Leah accumulated friends as they walked to the edge of the yard. Liz described what she had brought and where she had parked.

"We'll find your *Cara.* There aren't many here." Leah and her helpers bounced away.

"I forget how strange this must seem to you." Mary Ann's apologetic yet assuring smile lifted Liz's spirits a little. "My parents had close Amish friends, so we've felt comfortable together all my life. I thought you might like to experience their sense of community. Once you get over the culture shock, it's a special slice of Americana."

Liz smiled too. "Is there some way I can help? Maybe they—and I—would forget my strangeness if I could pitch in. I assume I can't help with the barn."

"You've got that right. They define male and female tasks very clearly."

"Yet I hesitate to invade Loretta's kitchen too." Besides, they might start yodeling again. Liz wanted to absorb her family's culture, but she couldn't handle the yodeling—at least, not today.

"The kids will start washing tables and benches soon for lunch. I'm sure they'd appreciate help. Their parents won't mind as long as we don't make them lazy." She winked.

"I doubt there's any danger of that." Flocks of children played in every corner of the farm. Older girls helped with cooking, picked early vegetables, and shepherded little ones. Older boys assisted with the grunt work of building the barn. They also cared for horses and took younger children for rides in pony carts, most of which did not exceed their mothers' speed limits. All the children seemed to consider themselves on call for any errands assigned by adults.

Liz tried to imagine them hunched over computers, playing video games, as Steve had done at that age.

She couldn't.

As Mary Ann had predicted, teen boys pulled wagons to the sycamore grove and began to unload wooden tables and benches. Liz couldn't understand their words, but she did remember a few things about teenage boys and easily interpreted their banter and veiled glances at the girls toting dishpans and dishrags. *Maybe Amish kids aren't so different after all.*

The girls' wide eyes studied Liz, but as they all washed tables and benches together, Mary Ann teased them into smiles. Liz told them about the inn and Beans's birthday party. Soon they were giggling as they scrubbed.

"The workers are making good progress on the barn." Mary Ann wrung out her cloth.

"'Good progress'?" Liz hooted. "If I hadn't watched this with my own two eyes, I wouldn't have believed it possible."

The men had completed the studwork and now lined up to hoist and secure huge panels at either end of the barn. An older man whose salt-and-pepper beard covered his barrel chest rarely raised his voice, but anyone watching knew he was in charge.

"That's Simeon Graber." Mary Ann read Liz's mind. "He leads most of the construction crews in Pleasant Creek. He manages them when they hire out too."

"He obviously knows his stuff." The work had not paused for a moment since Liz had arrived. This man had his large group working together like an intricate machine.

"Simeon's highly respected throughout the area." Mary Ann scrubbed at a stubborn spot on the table. "His family has served the Amish community for generations."

This hardworking model of virtue and the nasty, lecherous owner of a bankrupt company appeared to share little in common, other than the fact that both were builders. More than ever, Liz wished she knew more details about Peabody Construction and its connection to the Amish community. She doubted Gene Peabody would talk to her, but she'd try to contact him anyway. And at the next opportunity, she'd visit Countryside Commons.

"Those guys will be hungry." Mary Ann gestured toward the house. "Let's head to the kitchen. No one pays much attention to clocks, but I imagine they'll dish up soon."

Sure enough, they encountered an army of women and girls

carrying tablecloths, dishes, and silverware. They set tables with the same unerring precision as the men built the barn. Others carried trays of salt and pepper shakers, baskets of homemade bread, butter dishes, cream pitchers, and sugar bowls.

Ladies, wouldn't this be easier if you just raided a McDonald's or a pizza place?

No paper plates. No disposable silverware. Even the breakfasts that Liz prepared for her guests at the inn, in which she tried to avoid convenience foods and dishes, paled in comparison. Of course, Liz didn't have dozens of guests—or dozens of helpers either.

Liz trailed Mary Ann, who navigated the kitchen that seemed as crowded as a rock concert. She, along with other women, carried roasts, hams, and chicken with noodles to the serving tables, where they were distributed to the men. Liz lost track of the kinds of vegetables and salads she helped haul, and the cakes and pies she cut. All the while, she cast sideways glances at Simeon Graber. He wasn't a smiling man, but then, it didn't seem to her as if many Amish men were. Like the other ravenous workers, he focused on his food; still, he appeared affable and even laughed once. When approached with questions, he answered authoritatively. As Simeon rose from the table, his blue eyes happened to rest on Liz as she poured coffee nearby.

The moment froze both.

For one second? Maybe two? Then the moment was gone, and Simeon turned away to speak to his assistants again.

Her mind whirring like an old-fashioned clock, Liz poured more coffee. Simeon was a conservative of the conservatives. Perhaps an English woman's presence offended him.

But his look revealed more than that.

Recognition?

Yet she hadn't met him before.

Liz almost poured coffee on a man's pie plate instead of into his cup. Flushing, she replenished his drink and continued, cudgeling her brain as she tried to pinpoint Simeon's expression.

Recognition, yes. Unease. And amazement.

Why?

In that lined, placid Amish face, even momentary unease seemed as out of place as a pierced nose.

Liz continued down the table, but before she reached its end, most men had stood, readying for the afternoon's work. She helped clear plates while new supplies of food were carried out, and the women and children gathered at the tables. Famished, Liz ignored the June noonday heat and dug into a small mountain of noodles and mashed potatoes.

"I love eating with my Amish friends." Mary Ann heaped her plate high. "No one counts calories around here or talks about Weight Watchers. Or jogging."

Too hungry to reply, Liz let her former trainer's anti-carb monologue dribble out of her thoughts. But its exit only made more room for conjecture about Simeon and Clarence. Before she left, she should put out a feeler about Countryside Commons. Perhaps the tiniest wiggle of an innocuous bait might attract the beginning of an answer to the murder.

After splurging on sinfully rich chocolate cake and strawberry-rhubarb pie, Liz began to scrape and stack dishes.

"Hundreds of dishes!" Liz wiped her forehead. "Where will we wash them all?"

"Believe it or not, they already have a plan." Mary Ann pointed to another line of tables near the house and kettles of water bubbling over several large fires.

With the help of dozens of children, the women washed and dried. Liz's co-workers seemed to know whose dishes and pans belonged to whom.

She found herself working with teen girls again—a different group this time. A foreigner once more. For a while, she didn't try to shift the conversation from Swiss to English. Instead, she watched the men's progress. How had they covered the studs with full walls so fast? Now they were raising trusses to form the roof. Would they finish this barn by evening? She wished her Boston friends could share in this. Not only did these unassuming people accomplish this seemingly impossible task, they did it without electric tools or motors.

Did you come here to check out barn construction or get information that might help Isaac? Liz chided herself. If she was going to extend that feeler, she'd better do it soon, before they finished the dishes.

Liz guessed her teen group was exchanging the latest gossip as they washed and dried. Two wearing black Kapps teased the teens with white Kapps. Judging by blushing responses, Liz said, "Are any of you getting married soon?"

"Perhaps," several said. Their eyes shone.

One small brown-haired, pink-cheeked girl added, "Everyone must wait until after harvest before being published."

"Published?"

"That means the names of the couples and their wedding dates are announced in a special church meeting," Mary Ann, deep in soap suds at a neighboring table, explained. "Most weddings take place in November or December."

The brown-haired girl nodded. "This time next year, I hope to live in my own house."

"You are blessed, Hannah," one young woman said as she nudged her with a wet finger. "We lived three years with my parents before we could afford a home."

A small candle lit in Liz's mind. "Perhaps more work has been available this past year?"

Hannah nodded happily. "Mr. Graber's crews have been busier than usual, building in several counties."

Liz decided to take the plunge. "I heard they built several homes in Countryside Commons, near Fort Wayne."

"Yes. Jonathan said those houses were beautiful." Hannah clasped her hands.

"Big and expensive—which is why Hannah will have her own house next year," teased the married girl.

There is *a link between Clarence Peabody and Simeon Graber!*

The discovery only fomented more questions. Simeon and his workers apparently prospered because of the Countryside Commons deal. Why hadn't Clarence?

She could hardly wait to track down Gene Peabody's number on the Internet. Somehow, she would talk him into telling her more about his brother's company.

Even Liz's aching back and the prospect of more work waiting at the inn could not steal her anticipation.

Perhaps the truth would free Isaac, Miriam, and Sarah from this nightmare.

12

There was no answer at Gene Peabody's business number. Again.

Liz hesitated. *Should I leave a message?*

Instead, she pocketed her cell phone, opened the mini fridge in her private quarters, and poured herself a glass of peach tea. Catching Gene off guard might prove best. Given time, he would likely line up multiple reasons to refuse to talk to her.

Bone-tired from the barn raising, Liz forced her feet up the stairs to survey her next work projects. Upon checking the rooms, she breathed a silent blessing on Sarah. The girl hadn't wanted to attend the barn raising any more than Isaac's mother had; so instead, she'd worked her usual magic at the inn. She had waxed the beautiful old pine floor in the Somewhere in Time room and dusted the furniture within an inch of its life. Wall clocks, shelf clocks, mantel clocks—every glass surface gleamed a welcome, though she'd wound only Liz's favorite mantel clock, as the others were purely decorative. Of the wedding party soon to arrive, the bride's parents had selected this room—probably because her father appreciated the less feminine decor.

Sarah also had cleaned the Rose of Sharon room. Liz, having recently discovered Indiana author and naturalist Gene Stratton-Porter, included prints of her delicate flower and bird photos on the walls and graced the bookshelf with her novels. Two bridesmaids would share the room.

Two others would share the Amish room, restored to its patchwork-pillow and rag-rug cheeriness. She'd have Kiera pick daisies for that room tomorrow, just before the group arrived.

The bride, who wanted to get plenty of sleep before her wedding day, had decided to stay alone in the Sunset room on the third floor.

Liz added feminine frills—girly soaps, towels, and pillows to the room and bath to enhance its simple decor. Tomorrow she would transform the Heirloom room into a bridal suite for the newly wedded couple. Liz rechecked the inn's fridge and pantry, ran to the grocery store, and cleaned the living room and entry thoroughly.

Enough. She and Sarah would finish tomorrow. She realized she'd forgotten to call Gene Peabody again. Right now, she craved a soothing bath with lavender and then a quiet session alone on her bench reading her mother's diary—though she'd probably have to prop her eyelids open. She transferred the repeat phone call to tomorrow's to-do list.

An hour later, Liz stretched out on her bench, tucking a pillow behind her head. The retreating light would give her less than an hour to read outside, but she wanted to breathe in the evening's sweetness. Liz found her place in the diary and once more traveled back to share her mother's first Christmas in Boston.

As one of Santa's reindeer in a mall, Mom had unwittingly gained a front seat to all the wonders—and miseries—of an "English" Christmas.

Lights sparkled from every building, and colorful decorations transformed drab streets. The storybook, yet alien, beauty of the mall overwhelmed her as well as the children who stood in line to see Santa.

Why would a person hand over her child to a perfect stranger? her mother puzzled. *The tiny ones find Santa Claus frightening, not fun. They scream, but their parents pay for pictures anyway.*

Not surprisingly, her mom also struggled with the materialism, evident even back in 1971. *The children spout long lists of things they want. They do not ask for tops or dollies or wagons. Rather, they demand toys by name: Barbie, G.I. Joes, and . . . Hot Wheels? And what on earth is a Talking View-Master?*

Instead of becoming more reverent as Christmas approached, children and adults alike grew more impatient and greedy. Her mother wrote, *At home, we enjoyed small gifts and big family meals the day afterward, but Christmas Day itself involved prayer, fasting, and the reading of scripture. Perhaps it is too much to expect a spiritual emphasis at a mall. Few here seem to follow the Star to worship Christ. But then, I have known another who worships only his own star. He will do anything for personal gain.*

That star again. Liz sat up. *What did Mom mean? Who is this egotist who "worships only his own star"?* Drowsiness fled as she read the next pages about church services her mother attended. She found a small neighborhood church beautiful, with its piney Christmas greenery and candles. However, she almost fled when she realized men and women sat together in English churches.

More surprises awaited. The diary pages portrayed mingled delight and horror at instruments playing as congregations sang. Songs at Amish meetings were sung without accompaniment. The order of service, with much rising and sitting, intimidated her. Everyone but her seemed to know what to do when. Accustomed to two-hour sermons, she blinked when the pastor ended his after a mere half hour. But the healing words he spoke and scriptures he read about God's love and forgiveness through Christ nestled in a raw place in her heart. Despite the church's strangeness, she decided to return.

Liz's laughter and tears alternated as she read. Even after sunset forced her indoors, she continued reading late into the night. Valentine's Day, with its "invasion by an army of red hearts" bewildered her mother too. A note of deep loneliness made Liz wonder if her mom's departure had severed ties with a young man as well. Delight filled her as her mother adopted her church family, made friends at a new bakery job, and met Liz's father, Mark, when she ventured to a community college to take her first courses.

But her mom didn't mention the star again, nor the greedy man. Did she fear him as well?

Maybe I'm reading too much between the lines. Liz closed the diary and, turning off the central air, opened windows so the lullaby of night noises could sing her to sleep.

Such sweet quiet. Such peace. *Mom, why did you leave Pleasant Creek?*

The question might have kept her awake any other night, but the second Liz curled up atop her sheets, she fell asleep.

"This is Gene Peabody. Can I help you?"

Yes. But will you? Liz leaned against her small kitchen desk, gripping the phone. "Mr. Peabody, this is Liz Eckardt of Pleasant Creek, the owner of the Olde Mansion Inn. I attended your brother's funeral."

"I remember."

Liz matched his neutral tone. "The police may have told you they arrested an Amish boy, Isaac Borkholder, for murdering Clarence."

"Yes, they informed me." A slight edge had entered his voice.

Liz pushed on, "I'm a friend of Isaac's mother. He has other friends who share our opinion that he didn't commit this crime. We think he is protecting someone."

Silence.

"Mr. Peabody, would it be possible for you to meet with me? If the police understood a bit more about Clarence—"

"Are you from the police department?"

"No."

"I answered their questions." Now his voice grated on Liz. "If they need more information, why don't they ask for it themselves?"

"They—they think they have the right man." Liz gripped the phone with white knuckles. "But my friends and I believe new facts will point to someone else as the murderer."

"I don't have time for this," Gene growled. "I didn't know Clarence made me executor of his estate."

With access to all his business records. Now Liz *had* to talk him into a meeting. "I will keep it brief. Of course, I'll be glad to drive to Lafayette and meet you anywhere you wish."

Silence again.

Please, God. Please—

"All right. But only because you went to Clarence's funeral."

"Monday?" She couldn't let him think about it too long. "I can meet you for lunch or after work."

"Noon. The Blue Plate." He hung up.

Liz exhaled. Somehow, between now and Monday, she'd have to think up a subtle way to ask Gene about Countryside Commons. And about Simeon Graber.

Right. The Peabodys didn't appreciate subtlety. No matter what she said, Gene would cut to the chase.

Just how would she talk him into sharing Clarence's business records?

She still was pondering when Sarah approached. "The schedule says you want me to clean the kitchen this morning, right?"

"Yes, but don't push yourself too hard." Liz patted her shoulder. The girl's slightly plump, rosy cheeks had thinned almost daily. "Be sure to stop to eat lunch. Mary Ann brought a strawberry pie."

For the first time, Sarah's eyes lit up. "Lots of whipped cream?"

"Tons. This is one of Mary Ann's pies, remember?"

"I may have to sample that," Sarah said.

Ye-e-ss! Liz resisted the urge to pump her fist. Leave it to her knows-all, sees-all friend to bake just the thing to coax Sarah into eating. Smiling, Liz mounted the stairs and set her sights on transforming the Heirloom room into a bridal suite. She draped graceful lengths of white tulle around the enormous four-poster bed's light blue canopy. Liz added hand-tatted lace pillows to accent its antique pale blue coverlet. The white carved fireplace against a blue accent wall and the asymmetrical grouping of mirrors over the mantel helped make the room perfectly charming. A cushy contemporary sofa, antique furniture, and early 1900s Tiffany lamps blended well for a special-occasion, yet comfortable effect Liz hoped would make the couple feel at home.

Liz set vintage bride-and-groom photos around the room and two nineteenth-century goblets made by area glassblowers on the bedside table. She would add a chilled bottle of champagne, Swiss chocolates, and fresh flowers on the wedding day. She arranged handmade soaps and candles around the hot tub.

If only cleaning the inn were as much fun as decorating it.

Liz washed the four-season room's windows, dusted the furniture, and swept the floor. Kiera would arrange bouquets of roses, daisies, lilies, and wildflowers in pitchers and vases, distributing them throughout the inn.

The tanned, wiry girl was yanking weeds from the front yard's geranium beds as if dispatching mortal enemies. *How was I blessed with such amazing young helpers?*

All was well as long as she kept them apart.

Liz sighed, grabbed a big wedge of strawberry pie for lunch, and debated whether she should drop by Miriam's before the guests arrived. Mary Ann already had told the Amish woman about their jail visit. Liz had decided not to reveal her discoveries about Countryside Commons until she'd solidified more facts.

So why did she feel this urgency to visit Miriam today?

Just because. Though they might not share many words, she and Miriam somehow linked souls.

Liz jumped into her car and found the farm much faster this time. Nearing the Borkholders' place, she saw a covered buggy in the gravel driveway. Usually buggies around Pleasant Creek remained open throughout the year, and the Amish used huge black umbrellas in inclement weather. Also, during the busy summer, most Amish families went visiting on Sundays, not Thursdays. Perhaps she was interrupting a special family get-together. Liz almost turned around.

But when Miriam's smile welcomed her, Liz knew they were on the same page. Spending a few minutes in each other's company would lift their hearts.

Miriam gestured behind her. "Philip's aunts were about to join me on the porch." She introduced ninety-year-old Great-Aunt Beulah Borkholder, who had recently moved to a neighboring county to live near her second son. She and daughter-in-law Rachel wore one strip of muted flowered trim on their blue bodices, indicating their bishop held less stringent clothing standards than Pleasant Creek's. Had Great-Aunt Beulah built her retirement *Grossdawdy Haus* where she could enjoy more freedom?

Perhaps that explained why these ladies seemed comfortable in Liz's presence. Beulah was so comfortable, in fact, that she nodded off while sitting in the wooden swing.

"She thought today was Sunday," Rachel whispered. "Arguing does little good. I hope you don't mind that I brought her."

"Not at all. Aunt Beulah helped so much when my children were small. You've brightened my day." Miriam emphasized her last sentence. Liz wondered if her local relatives had quietly drawn back from the Borkholders because of Isaac—not shunning, but a distancing that had added to their burden.

They exchanged pleasantries, mostly about Rachel's family and her daughter Doris's marriage prospects. Finally, a widower was courting Doris. He was fifteen years older, with five children, but at thirty, she couldn't expect to marry a man her own age.

A slight sweat broke out on Liz's forehead. She honored her Amish roots, but she certainly didn't understand all their ways. *Doris, I hope you enjoy a challenge.*

Chitchat of a possible October wedding, however, eased Miriam's tension. Liz watched the lines in her friend's face relax, until Rachel rose to leave.

"We were so sorry to hear of Isaac's troubles."

Miriam paled, but she nodded. "Thank you."

Rachel said with sudden vehemence, "I wish that Peabody had never set foot in Pleasant Creek."

"Peabody? Clarence Peabody?" Great-Aunt Beulah raised her head, foggy blue eyes suddenly lucid. "He was here awhile, working for his *Grossvater* on that fancy house downtown. Long time ago."

"Ja, Mutter." Chagrined, Rachel helped her mother-in-law to her feet. "It's time for us to go—"

"English," the old woman mused as they all walked to their buggy. "Enoch Yoder wouldn't let him court his daughter Mattie, of course. She was one of my youngest daughter's best friends. Felt a little sorry for the boy—heard he wouldn't eat for days."

Yoder? The name caught Liz's attention as if on a hook. As in Sarah Yoder? Or one of the many other Yoders in Pleasant Creek?

Her mind filed away the information for later. She joined in waving goodbye as the buggy rolled away.

Liz glanced at her phone. Her guests would arrive around the usual three thirty check-in time, but she'd grab a few more minutes with Miriam before leaving—if her friend acquiesced.

Miriam's barely visible head gesture toward the porch confirmed Liz's hope. Walking together, Liz remembered she'd wanted to ask Miriam about the stars on Amish barns. Perhaps an off-topic question might distract her friend's thoughts. "I love the star designs I've seen on barns here. Do they have some special significance?"

"No. They are simply decoration." Miriam pointed to her own unadorned white barn. "Our bishop does not forbid them, but he dislikes them. Philip and I do not mind following his wishes."

For a while, they shared drowsy quiet as buzzing bees went about their business among Miriam's roses. Liz wished this moment could last forever.

It didn't.

Miriam's calm faded. She drew a trembling breath. "We must trust in Gött. He will do what He will do."

"Yes." If Miriam felt like talking, Liz would let her. Still, she could not help saying, "But I believe God wants justice too. You're aware

Mary Ann and I visited Isaac? I don't think he killed Mr. Peabody."

"But his fingerprints were on the awl." Miriam brushed a tear that finally had escaped her eye. "He was there at the lake. He lied to Philip and me about going to meet Sarah." Her voice faded to a frail whisper. "Why would *mein Sön* do such things?"

Liz took her hand. "Perhaps he is protecting someone."

"But that is not our way." Miriam raised her chin. "Lies protect no one. Only Gött can truly protect His own."

Liz had no answer for that. She squeezed her friend's hand while Miriam wiped tears with her apron.

Finally, Liz said, "I'm praying for Isaac. And for you and your family."

"Thank you." Miriam brushed her apron as if trying to wipe sadness from her life.

"We appreciate your prayers." Philip's deep voice jolted their hands apart. Dark brows hunched over his opaque eyes.

You don't look as if you appreciate them. "I am so sorry for all your family is going through," Liz stammered.

"It is made worse for my wife by outsiders." Miriam's husband did not raise his voice, but its firmness rivaled that of his house's stone foundation. "The reporters, the tourists who treat killing as if it is entertainment for their sake. They all injure our family further."

"Philip, Liz is a friend." Miriam's gentle rebuke set a distinct boundary for her husband's anger.

Though the man's handsome face under his beard betrayed no weakness, Liz could believe he suffered with his son's tribulation as well.

"I should go." Liz squeezed Miriam's hand again and turned toward her car. Perhaps, when Miriam stopped by Sew Welcome for supplies, they could share a few moments together in Liz's private quarters.

She paused a second to tell Miriam's roses goodbye. Unless a miracle cleared up this mess, Philip's glare told Liz she and Miriam had enjoyed their last afternoon on her friend's porch.

13

"What a gorgeous old house!"

"I'm *so* glad we're staying here."

The wedding group's delighted exclamations raised Liz's spirits as she welcomed them and showed them their rooms. As Bob Meisner, the portly father of the bride, hauled his wife's extensive luggage into the Somewhere in Time room, the antique German mantel clock chimed four.

"Mary Ann was right about lodging here in Pleasant Creek." Sherry, the bride's mother, oohed and aahed as she toured the second-story rooms. "I wish I could stay in every room!"

"Is Mary Ann related to you?" Liz asked.

"She's my cousin." Sherry grinned. "But we've always been like sisters. She used to get me in trouble all the time."

"I can believe that." If Mary Ann the teenager bore any resemblance to Mary Ann the adult, Sherry was fortunate to have survived.

Tara, Sherry's red-haired daughter, and her bridesmaids inspected the Heirloom room. Tara shrugged off their teasing and thanked Liz, her eyes shining. "It's perfect. These wonderful little touches make it so special."

"You're welcome." *This bunch will be fun.* Liz continued, "Inn guests share coffee, lemonade, and cookies at this time each day. You're all welcome to join us downstairs."

Naomi had outdone herself in making wedding cookies. The beautifully detailed silver and white hearts with the bride's and groom's initials charmed everyone—and *mmm*, did they taste good!

"Too bad the guys are missing this," the maid of honor said, blissfully chomping her third cookie.

"Lots more for us." Tara licked away icing with a seeming lack of conscience. She told Liz the groom and his friends were staying at a nearby lake cottage. "I hope Michael and the other guys get their craziness out of their systems tomorrow."

"It would be just like them to stay out all night after the rehearsal dinner and show up late to the wedding," a bridesmaid said.

"No way." Tara's mischievous smile widened. "Michael's mother promised they'd get up. She said she'd use water pistols, if necessary."

Sherry grinned. "Did you bring one for me?"

Hanging out with the laid-back, funny group, Liz almost forgot about the difficult end to her visit with Miriam and Great-Aunt Beulah's reference to Clarence Peabody.

Almost. After the group left to decorate the country church where the ceremony would take place, Liz carried dishes to the kitchen and pondered the old Amish lady's comments. Was Enoch Yoder, who'd vetoed Clarence Peabody's romance with his daughter, related to Sarah? If so, did that family connection have anything to do with Peabody's murder? Maybe Liz could run down to the courthouse tomorrow after breakfast and learn more.

Speaking of breakfast, I'd better check our supplies again. The wedding brunch, which would also include the groom, his parents, and groomsmen, would require far more than pastries, eggs, and fruit—plus plenty of help. For an infinitesimal moment, Liz considered using both Sarah and Kiera to serve and clean up.

No way. So far, they hadn't repeated their earlier clash, but Liz would not gamble an important event on a mere hope that the cat and the dog would play nice. Maybe one of the Material Girls would help out Saturday morning. She stopped by Sew Welcome to ask.

"Of course, I will. Tara's my second cousin." Mary Ann looked as thrilled as if Liz had handed her a $500 bill.

"Are you sure? You're going to the wedding too."

"I'm sure."

"I'll be out of town for a few days." Sadie clucked her regret. "My niece just got out of the hospital."

"We'll miss you." Mary Ann patted her arm and Liz's too. "Now, don't you worry about a thing. Opal will help too. Or Caitlyn."

Liz shook her head as she left Sew Welcome. Mary Ann, who freely volunteered her friends' services, got away with it because she delighted in running other people's lives almost as much as she enjoyed helping.

Enoch Yoder *was* related to Sarah. Liz, having stolen an hour at the county courthouse, stared at blotted handwriting on the county birth records. Jeremiah Yoder, Sarah's father, was Enoch's grandson, and Sarah, his great-granddaughter. Enoch's daughter Mattie, now deceased, had been Jeremiah's aunt. Perhaps Sarah resembled Mattie in her youth? Maybe, in attempting to romance Sarah, Peabody was trying to relive happy times he'd shared with his lost love.

Jeremiah Yoder. Liz paused, her finger on his name. She hadn't considered Sarah's father as Clarence's possible killer. Like Isaac, he no doubt loathed the construction company owner who chased first his aunt and then his daughter. Had rage hidden behind Jeremiah's calm demeanor?

Had the police checked his alibi? Liz had already asked Chief Houghton about Sarah's, and she couldn't question the chief about every possible suspect . . .

Isaac's arrest had occurred so quickly, so conveniently. But would he lie to protect his future father-in-law?

Surely not. But then, she couldn't imagine Isaac killing anyone either.

Though faulty air-conditioning kept the dusty old office steamy, a chill froze Liz to the creaky chair. This murder had devastated everyone concerned. Would its sinister influence spread even further? It posed such a contrast to the inn's happy atmosphere this weekend. Glancing at her phone, Liz realized she'd spent more time at the courthouse than she'd planned. The wedding party wasn't due back for another hour, but Liz wanted to prepare for coffee hour and stay available. As she left the courthouse's musty, marbled interior, the afternoon's sunny rays chided her concerns. Chief Houghton was obviously an experienced policeman. Surely he'd confirmed Jeremiah's whereabouts during the time of the murder.

Still, Sarah's drawn face and the black circles under her dulled eyes floated through Liz's thoughts. Miriam's sad but resolute mouth and raised chin replayed again and again as Liz walked home. Like a bird with no nest, her mind flitted from Isaac to Jeremiah to . . . whom?

Did she really want to find out who had killed Clarence Peabody?

"Oh, Tara." Liz clasped her hands as she stood, along with the bridesmaids, at the bottom of the stairs. "You look so lovely."

Sherry dabbed at her eyes as her daughter embraced her. The girls echoed Liz's admiration as Tara made her way slowly down the steps. Even Beans raised an eyelid at her descent, his tail wagging twice.

In keeping with the 1860s clapboard country church and her career as a history teacher, Tara and her wedding party wore clothing that reflected the period. Her white lawn-fabric dress featured a hoopskirt, delicately fashioned bodice, with many tucks and buttons and sheer narrow lace sleeves. Shining red hair fell almost to her waist, covered with a flowing veil attached to a crown of white blossoms. She carried a bouquet of white lilies, roses, and greenery. The attendants wore dove-gray dresses with matching bonnets, accented with pink ribbons. They carried nosegays of pink and magenta roses. Liz had to remind herself to take pictures—the first wedding photos in her inn's album.

"Thanks for all your help." Tara squeezed Liz's hand and turned to her bridesmaids. "I'm glad we practiced walking in hoopskirts!"

Thank goodness the Olde Mansion Inn's front entrance seemed to have been designed for women wearing voluminous dresses.

Bob Meisner was struck speechless at the sight of his daughter. His Victorian tails, top hat, and walking stick gave him a distinguished look. He kissed Tara and then Sherry, who wore an elegant vintage pink silk dress and straw bonnet, helping them into a waiting buggy. Another hired buggy picked up the other girls.

Snapping photos, Liz laughed. So much fun! Perhaps she should be paying the Meisners! As the horses pulled buggies out of her driveway, though, she mentally celebrated the fact the reception would take place elsewhere. Everyone's room keys opened the front door, so they could return at any hour. After tidying rooms, she anticipated no major tasks until brunch tomorrow. Liz poured herself a cup of raspberry tea, grabbed the last wedding cookie, and plunked onto a chair in the four-season room to relish a few lazy moments.

Her cell phone rang. Sighing, Liz set down her tea and answered.

"Hello, Liz?" The woman's voice sounded familiar. "This is Emily Hart. I'll be in Indianapolis for a meeting on Monday, but I'd rather stay with you afterward. Do you, by any chance, have a single room open?"

Her first return guest! "The Sunrise room is available."

"Perfect. May I show up around five?"

Quickly, Liz calculated her driving time after meeting with Gene. "I'm driving back from Lafayette that afternoon, but I should make it back before then."

"Don't hurry. A tenderloin at Mama's Home Cooking is already calling my name."

Liz heard the grin in Emily's tone. "Okay. I'll take my time."

Liz hung up. She'd hoped for a break, but a return guest meant a growing reputation for the inn, plus a little unexpected income to add to the off-season savings account.

Besides, Emily rated near the top of her easy-to-please list.

Liz decided to join Kiera in the potting shed, replacing wilting bouquets and readying vases of lilies and roses for the bridal suite. The girl was a treasure, definitely worth the cost of her increased hours.

"Someday, when I get married, I'd love flowers like these." Kiera's rough fingers handled the blossoms with tenderness.

So the taciturn teen did harbor delicate dreams beyond the hard life she rarely mentioned. Liz gave in to impulse. "If you're still around here, we'll make that happen."

The smile that rewarded Liz went directly into her mental "don't ever forget this" file. *As if I could.*

Afterward, Liz enjoyed a quick swim, sunbathed on the pier, and then retreated to the inn's cool recesses to once more try to finish reading her thriller. But a giant tenderloin sandwich at Mama's also called her name. Another post-dinner reading session relaxed Liz into a cricket-song bedtime. *I wish I'd moved here twenty years ago.* Just as she drifted to sleep, a loud noise sounded.

Clang-clang-clang-clang!

Liz leaped from her bed. A fire?

Rattle-rattle-rattle, CLANG! Rattle-rattle CLANG!

Cowbells sounded too, along with slide whistles and people singing at the top of their lungs.

Mardi Gras? In Pleasant Creek? Liz stumbled to the window and pressed her nose against the screen. At first, she saw little in the darkness. Then she realized the psycho band and chorus were milling around the inn's yard.

She glanced at her bedside clock. 1:35 a.m.

I don't have to deal with this, whatever it is. That's what police are for. She grabbed her phone and speed-dialed the police chief.

"What's going on, Ms. Eckardt?" Houghton's concerned, down-to-earth tone reassured her.

"I don't know. I think these people have had too much to drink. But why they came here, I have no idea!"

"Who are 'these people'?"

"The ones banging and yelling outside. They're wandering around the yard."

"Yeah, I can hear 'em." The chief's voice had lost its edge. "Are you hosting a wedding?"

What does that have to do with anything? "We have a wedding party staying here, yes."

"Bride and groom too?"

Did she hear a *smile* in his voice? "Yes."

"Welcome to rural Indiana, Ms. Eckardt. Don't have them as often as we used to, but they still happen." He chuckled. "What you've got going is a shivaree."

"A what?" Liz strained to hear above the uproar.

"A shivaree. The bride and groom's friends show up on their wedding night and make a ruckus. It's usually harmless, unless things get out of control."

Clang-clang-rattle-rattle . . . How did he define "out of control"?

"If you see excessive alcohol passed around, or the noise doesn't settle down within a half hour or so, call me back. I'll clear 'em out for you."

Liz gripped her now-throbbing temple. A half hour? After she hung up, she'd set her stopwatch.

"One more thing . . . they usually expect the host to let 'em in and feed 'em a little something." He hung up, laughing outright.

Clang-clang-rattle-rattle-rattle, BAM, BAM, BAM!

Mary Ann's voice bellowed from just outside her window. "Liz, are you awake?"

Liz tried not to swear. She yelled, "What do you think?"

A howl of laughter greeted her.

Mary Ann yelled back, "The girls and I stowed goodies for everybody in the pantry. They're in the plastic containers in the back cabinets. You want to let us in?" She rang her cowbell with her usual boundless enthusiasm.

In a word, no. "You've got a key. Why don't you let them in?"

"That would be rude!"

More laughter.

Peering out the window, Liz spotted Tara and her new husband exchanging fun jibes with their tormentors. If they participated in this bizarre ritual, Liz supposed she, as hostess, should too. But what about Sherry and Bob, who had paid for this weekend?

Liz threw on jeans and a T-shirt. Debating whether she should knock on their door, she opened hers—and found a note taped to it. *Bob and Sherry are staying at Sadie's house.*

The note was in Mary Ann's handwriting. Leave it to her to cover all the bases. Had Sadie been informed of this arrangement? What if she came home early from her trip?

Liz hurried to the open front door. She tapped on Tara's shoulder. "You want to invite them in?"

The bride laughed, though she looked a little tired. "Oh, we're fine with it. The choice is totally up to you. But they say they won't leave until they get something to eat."

"I can do that." Liz flashed an A-OK sign and hastened to the pantry as the crowd poured in. Liz didn't mind scoring unwarranted hostess-with-the-mostest points.

Whoa. The Material Girls had been at work. Liz uncovered big trays of crackers, breads, more wedding cookies, and fruit, which she set on the dining room table. She fired up the coffeepot and found pitchers of punch and tea, as well as plates of cheese, hidden behind milk jugs in her refrigerator. But then Mary Ann, Naomi, Opal, and Caitlyn scurried in and kicked her out of her kitchen. "Okay, you're done here. We're taking over for the rest of the night."

Liz didn't argue for a second. She joined the partygoers, who exclaimed at all the goodies, toasting Tara and Michael and celebrating another couple who had become engaged at the reception. Having left cowbells and other noisemakers in the foyer, the group's rowdy levels dropped considerably, and Liz even detected a few yawns. Within an hour, the inn's lower story had cleared.

Sweet quiet. Almost.

"Just you wait, Mary Ann." Tara eyed her grinning relative. "When you get married again, look out!"

"You're the ones who'll have to wait," Mary Ann said placidly. "A long, long time."

"Oh, we'll introduce you to the perfect guy." Michael pulled his wife into an embrace. "Someone like me."

Everyone chuckled, and the couple headed upstairs. Liz faced her friends, lined up by the kitchen. She crossed her arms. "I don't know whether to thank you all or clobber you."

"Come on, you enjoyed our little initiation, didn't you?" Mary Ann wheedled.

"You do this to everyone who moves here from the city?" Liz tried to frown.

"Only people we really like." Mary Ann took Liz's empty coffee cup. "Oh, just so you know, I changed the sheets in the Sunset room. Naomi and I are sleeping here so we can get up with you tomorrow morning to help with the brunch."

At least she told me this time. Liz trudged wearily to her bedroom. If Mary Ann had popped out of the woodwork at the crack of dawn, the Olde Mansion Inn might be saddled with another murder. And there would be no mystery about that whodunit.

No mystery at all.

14

Pumped up by listening to *Girls Just Want to Have Fun*—one of her mom's favorite songs—on the radio and by the highway breezes from her open car window, Liz's heart lifted. This meeting with Gene Peabody might actually work out!

Maybe the newly engaged couple's reservation for next April had added to her good mood. Plus, the help she'd received from the Material Girls yesterday had culminated in a flawless brunch for her departing guests and a spotless inn from top to bottom, giving Liz time to relax.

Unfortunately, in cleaning the living room, Mary Ann had noticed the absence of Liz's mother's portrait on the fireplace mantel. Now Liz shifted behind the wheel, a small finger of disquiet niggling through her cheerfulness.

"Do you have relatives in Indiana?" Mary Ann had asked. "Did you visit here as a child?"

Liz had answered, "None that I know of," and bustled out to vacuum the dining room. If Mary Ann discovered her quest for her mother's family, would all of Pleasant Creek hear about it by nightfall? The Amish community, who especially censored dissenters like Abigail, might shut out Liz forever.

Mary Ann lived like a neon sign. And if Mary Ann was a neon sign, Sadie was a stadium big screen. Liz groaned.

If only she could speed up her personal investigation. But with all the unsolved details of Peabody's murder, how could she find time to conduct her family research?

Slow down, Liz. A speeding ticket wouldn't accomplish her goals.

By the time she pulled into The Blue Plate, a mom-and-pop restaurant on Lafayette's outskirts, her earlier beach-ball buoyancy had sprung a slow leak. Despite the cashier's friendly greeting and the restaurant's homey red-and-white tablecloths, Gene's pointed politeness deflated her further.

The bearlike man, wearing dark green work clothes, dumped salt on his double cheeseburger and french fries. "I'm not sure what I can do to help you, Ms. Eckardt."

"Actually, I'm hoping to help you, Mr. Peabody." Liz nibbled her Cobb salad. "I'm sorry you lost your brother, and I want justice done."

"S'pose it did happen in your backyard." He cast a hard look at her. "Probably didn't do your business any good."

Well, I thought *he wasn't as mean as Clarence.* Liz planed anger from her voice. "On the contrary, it's generated tons of publicity, though not the kind I'd want. We're booked every long weekend through October, as well as some weekdays."

Gene grunted. "Oh? Good."

Good? Gene's mixed signals were hard to interpret, but then, grief did make people crazy in different ways. Liz said carefully, "Could you tell me a little about Clarence, about his business?" *About your partnership?*

"Not much to tell." He took a mammoth bite but chewed with no dribbles or noise.

Liz waited.

He swallowed. "As kids, Clarence and I worked summers with our dad in his construction company. As he got older, we became partners. I'm better at the business side of building. Clarence was like Dad, a builder at heart."

Liz remembered his acid warning about altering Olde Mansion Inn's historic structure. Apparently, his rudeness had camouflaged true passion for architecture.

"Sounds like you made a winning combination."

"We did well enough." Gene paused. "Until Clarence started kicking against what I knew was best for us."

So, you knew what was best? She didn't have to imagine Clarence's reaction to that.

"This company out of Chicago, Midwest Services, wanted to partner with us on some projects. Had an Amish front man. Met him couple of times—name was Abe Brenneman." Lightning flashed across Gene's stormy eyes.

Whoa. Liz resisted the urge to flatten herself against the blue vinyl booth. She nodded, afraid one word would make him clam up.

"When he listened to that guy more than me, I knew I couldn't stay." Gene thumped his glass of soda, shaking the table. "Haven't had time to go through Clarence's stuff yet, but I bet that Amish buzzard picked his bones clean. Lawyer's been bugging me for records, said Clarence filed bankruptcy. But I'm not gonna just hand over everything."

You didn't know? Perhaps the brothers hadn't spoken since the split. Now it was too late. Liz said slowly, "Did Clarence or his lawyer mention anything about a housing project called Countryside Commons?"

"No," Gene spat. "He didn't mention anything."

She decided not to probe further. "I know how difficult it is to go through a deceased relative's belongings. I lost my mother recently and had to take care of a ton of details afterward."

At the mention of her mother's death, Gene's eyes softened. "I'm sorry you lost your mama."

"Thank you." *Grief unites us all.* "Trying to track someone else's life can be pretty confusing. I'd be glad to help you examine Clarence's records and see exactly what happened."

Relief and gratitude washed across Gene's face—until a trickle of suspicion lowered his bushy brows. "Why? Are you a lawyer or something?"

He spoke the word "lawyer" as if it were synonymous with "scum."

Liz looked him in the eye. "I was a patent lawyer in Boston before I came to Pleasant Creek. But I don't have a license to practice in Indiana. I help friends strictly on a pro bono basis."

The damage already had been done, it seemed. Gene shook his head. "Clarence has caused me enough trouble without draggin' in a lawyer I don't know from Adam—or Eve. I'm not even sure why I came here today." He pushed back his half-finished plate with an air of finality and glared at her.

"Maybe because you realize that I care. Because you know that I want justice for your brother, for a twenty-year-old boy stuck in jail, and for his mother, who can't save him." She stood and placed her business card on the table. "Thank you for your time, Mr. Peabody. If you change your mind, please let me know."

At least she'd pried a few clues from Gene. That night, Liz readily found Midwest Services' Web page, with its advertisement of residential and business construction. But it listed only an address on Chicago's south side and an email address. There was no personnel or phone number. She emailed, asking for an appointment. Then she checked the address on her phone's GPS, which she had named Lavinia because of its aristocratic voice. Liz thought she could drive to Chicago and back in one day, leaving a full day to prepare for guests' arrivals on Thursday. She could study the company anonymously before she made actual contact with its management.

She was still debating the next morning when she served Emily the continental breakfast she'd requested.

"Wish I could stay longer," the librarian said, "but I have to go home."

"I'm glad you have the perfect day for driving." Liz's urge to visit Midwest Services doubled as she thought of the clues she might unearth, and as she wrinkled her nose at cleaning her own messy quarters or laundering piles of towels and sheets. "I'm trying to decide whether to go to Chicago or not."

"Getting away is nice." Emily grinned. "I heard you had a busy weekend."

By the end of their conversation, Liz had convinced herself to go. She grabbed bottles of water, patted Beans good-bye, and jumped into her car. Taking the interstate, Liz soon zoomed her way through acres of farmland and forest to Chicago's outskirts, where Lavinia directed her to an exit. Too excited to grab lunch, Liz followed her GPS's map through blue-collar neighborhoods and older strip malls to an industrial area. She'd expected this less-than-scenic change as she approached her destination. Nevertheless, she rechecked her car's locks.

Come on, Liz. You lived in the city most of your life. Had Pleasant Creek's quaint downtown and lovely streets already spoiled her? No more than its friendly people.

Now Liz had entered a rundown twilight zone. The few people she saw regarded her with hostile glances. Worse yet, some gazed with keen interest at her car. *What was I thinking?*

"Well, Lavinia, this is one fine mess you've gotten us into," she told the GPS.

"Recalculating," said Lavinia.

Liz winced. Okay, if she herself had done more recalculating in the first place, she would have rented an economy sedan with a dent in its side.

Today, however, she *would* find Midwest Services at 837 West Appleton Avenue. She wound through pothole-riddled streets that often morphed into alleys. Lavinia directed her to one road that disappeared altogether. Finally, Liz found West Appleton Avenue.

She pulled up in front of a small vacant building that in its former life might have been a business. Its faint street number read 837. Behind it, a crumbling brick warehouse with rows of painted windows near its roof looked as if it had been deserted decades before.

Unseen stares from behind shades and around corners fastened on Liz like invisible tentacles. She tried to shrug herself free.

Still, Liz forced herself to park. Gripping her pepper spray, she walked to the smaller building and peered through the smeary, cracked front windows. Empty. Plaster, fallen from a gaping hole in the ceiling, covered the brown broken-tile floor. From the looks of the mess, no one had disturbed it for months, perhaps years.

Liz cast a look back at the Acura. It still possessed all its tires and hubcaps. Should she risk its well-being—and possibly her own—to look inside the warehouse, if she could enter? The windows were located too high for her to catch a glimpse of the interior.

The warehouse appeared as deserted as its office building, but Midwest Services might have used it in some capacity.

Liz walked around the office to what to be the appeared the warehouse's main entrance.

Voilà!

She ran her fingers over the outline of letters interposed on a hammer-shaped logo resembling the one on the Midwest Services' website. Though only fragments of the letters could be detected, she easily could deduce a capital *M* and an *S*. Surely the company had used this warehouse! And judging from the clarity of the logo's outline, it had been removed only recently.

Having stuffed the pepper spray into her pocket, Liz couldn't budge the weather-beaten but solid front door. A side door was locked as well. A sagging back door boasted a padlock, but when she rattled it, the corroded hinges gave way, leaving a not-quite-big-enough gap. Using a jagged piece of metal she retrieved from a nearby rubbish pile, she pushed the door open and squeezed inside the warehouse.

A room that looked like a big, shadowy cave stretched before her, relieved by a few suppressed sunbeams. She couldn't identify the dilapidated wooden and metal structures scattered here and there.

Tons of trash, shredded cardboard packaging, split pallets, and broken glass littered the floor. Liz retrieved a small flashlight from her bag and scanned the floor for . . . what? She didn't know.

The room didn't give her the same deserted-forever impression the office building did. There weren't nearly as many spiderwebs and, fortunately, no musty, choking atmosphere or dank, decaying stink. She could inhale somewhat normally—

A sound.

Was it a footstep?

Now Liz's pulse echoed in her ears, its beat seeming to bounce off the filthy walls.

She hunkered down behind one of the broken machines and waited. She heard nothing.

Nothing?

She listened, every tendon of her body stretched taut as wire.

Again.

It wasn't a rustle. It wasn't a nibble.

It was just an indefinable noise that told her someone else was there.

Someone was watching her.

A choice hovered in her brain. Fight or flee? Clasping her pepper spray again, she launched herself forward. Her feet skimmed the littered floor. She pushed her way through the door into the bright sunlight and dashed to her car.

"Lady, you need help?" A tall man standing in front of the

dilapidated yellow house across the street welded his gaze to Liz. His features looked boyish. His smirk was not.

"No, thanks." She punched her "unlock" button and yanked on her car's door handle.

Still locked.

He was crossing the street. Two others joined him.

She punched again. *Please. Open. Please—*

The locks clicked. She slammed herself into the car and started the engine. It peeled out as if it, too, feared for its life.

This time Lavinia cooperated, guiding Liz out of the neighborhood and pinpointing a family restaurant near the interstate where Liz could leave her car without a bodyguard. She parked close to the front door and played a soothing Haydn quartet for a few minutes.

"Stop shaking," she ordered her muscles. "Stop it now."

For a while, neither her voice nor muscles obeyed. Finally, she ventured from the car. After buying a map at a nearby filling station, she pored over it and scavenged the Internet while devouring a Gene-sized double cheeseburger at the restaurant. After scrutinizing every road in the Chicago area and endless lists of businesses, she confirmed what she had seen: Midwest Services no longer existed in Chicago.

But who had been watching as she explored the warehouse? A homeless person hoping she wouldn't order him out of his only shelter? Perhaps a family of rats, foraging for the day's meal? Liz recalled her panicked race out the door. A flush of embarrassment crawled up her cheeks.

But her spectator could have been a junkie, or some equally dangerous person.

On the other hand, maybe the guys who offered their "help," actually wanted to.

No. She hadn't misinterpreted their hungry gazes. They wanted her car, her money, her, or all three. Had their creepy friend chased her from the warehouse into their clutches?

Massaging her tight forehead, she fled from those thoughts and turned a different direction.

When had Midwest Services moved—and why?

15

Did Liz ever want to leave Pleasant Creek again?

As when she first visited, her blood pressure dropped five points merely in passing the town limits sign. It fell to normal levels as she unlocked the inn's back door and kicked off her sandals.

Peach tea and a comfy seat on the front porch completed her transformation.

Aaah . . . Hundreds of fireflies lit tiny lanterns in the falling dusk. One car passed and then, eventually, another. Somebody waved; Liz waved back.

It was so different from the two-hour traffic jam that had clogged the interstate on the way home, not to mention the disaster zone of Appleton Avenue. She chuckled ruefully. It had such a storybook name, but it was such a scary place. For this evening, she would attempt to put it out of her mind.

Procrastination felt good. She didn't want to enter her messy quarters. A light breeze perfumed with the petunia beds' fragrance coaxed her to stay put. She inhaled the summer night. "Maybe I'll sleep out here on the chaise."

Liz might have done it—except for Peabody's murder. She sighed as she rose to leave. How many other Pleasant Creek citizens were taking extra precautions because of the ugly incident?

Liz pulled mail from the antique mailbox by the front steps and, once inside, locked doors and deadbolts. She flipped on lights and riffled through a handful of bills and flyers. A thank-you card from Sherry and Bob Meisner caught her eye. She smiled. Shivaree and all, that wedding weekend shone as the highlight of her inn ownership—so far. Would the other four weddings scheduled prove as much fun?

One envelope bore no addresses or stamp. Only her name in capital letters. Perhaps it held a check from Mary Ann and Sadie? But they'd already paid this month's rent.

She opened the envelope and examined the cheap notebook paper with its few printed lines. They looked like German, or some Amish dialect. She recognized the word *Gött*, but nothing else. No one had signed it.

What did it mean? Did it have anything to do with the murder? Who sent it?

Hackles rising, Liz entered her sitting room and dropped onto the still-messy sofa. After driving for hours, only to be chased out of Chicago by the Appleton Avenue Gang, she deserved a break. Liz considered running the letter through the shredder.

Yet she longed to understand its meaning. If only she could ask Miriam. Or Sarah. Before Liz completed the thought, she was shaking her head.

Even if her closest Amish friends weren't embroiled in this murder, she couldn't ask anyone around Pleasant Creek. Her question would only create a hundred more she didn't want to answer.

The writer mostly likely was awaiting her reaction. She wouldn't give him the satisfaction. But who *was* the writer?

Simeon Graber? She recalled his apprehensive expression at the barn raising. Surely, he wasn't trying to scare her away from Pleasant Creek just because she'd crashed a barn party. Perhaps he simply disapproved of her and was warning her of God's disapproval.

Philip? He seemed to regard her as one of the outsiders upsetting his wife, Miriam.

Liz dug her nails into her now-throbbing head. The more she sought to untangle this mystery, the more threads looped their way into the mess.

She tucked the note into a file, took a couple of headache tablets, and stretched out on her bed. She'd send the letter to a translation service tomorrow. End of story—at least, until she knew the facts, rather than the fiction her weary brain was inventing.

Closing her eyes, however, didn't end the story. Even drifting off into an exhausted sleep sent Liz on journeys into gloomy buildings full of leering street guys and piles of Amish books all written by authors named Lavinia.

"Does that girl ever wear anything that isn't torn or faded?" Sadie, watching Kiera water backyard flowers from Sew Welcome's workroom windows, turned to Liz as if she chose the teen's wardrobe. "Her clothes don't fit either. They either hang on her like a tent or are way too small."

"She does mostly yard work. No big deal." Liz trimmed the seams in her quilt block—almost too closely. "Sometimes, though, I've seen her downtown on her days off, and she wears the same outfits. Is it a teen thing?"

"No." Caitlyn bit off a thread. "Sure, kids wear torn jeans and stuff. But Kiera's look doesn't say, 'I'm cool.' It says, 'I'm poor.'"

Liz winced. "She doesn't talk much about her home life. Still, I've caught several hints that she spends her money on her younger siblings."

"Her tennies have holes in them," Mary Ann pointed out.

"I know." Liz sighed. "I've thought of offering to buy her new ones, but I'm not sure she'd welcome my help."

"That does complicate matters, doesn't it?" Opal looked up from the ironing board. "But I'm glad she possesses some sense of independence."

"She has plenty of that." Liz grinned.

Naomi paused in embroidering an appliqué. "What if . . . ?"

"Oh, no." Mary Ann rolled her eyes. "Naomi's going to stick us with a new project."

Liz didn't know whether to laugh or groan. *Naomi?* Mary Ann dipped a finger in every local pie and, without conscience, conscripted the Material Girls to do likewise.

Unperturbed, Naomi continued, "What if we helped establish a local fund for kids like Kiera? Or we could check with the school system to see if a similar kids' clothing fund is already in place. Perhaps they'd welcome partners from the community." She tapped her fingers on the long worktable. "We'll soon finish our fall quilt; we could begin another and raffle it off, benefitting that fund. And we could ask local businesses to contribute."

The other Material Girls chimed in enthusiastic approval, but Liz hesitated. "Would that approach make it acceptable to teens like Kiera?"

"I'll bet it would, if she participates in making the quilt," Naomi said. "If teens want to join us in sewing projects to benefit the fund, we can teach them beginning skills."

"How many teens?" Caitlyn's eyebrows rose. "I'd love to help, but we only have so much time and space."

"Two or three per project," Naomi answered.

Caitlyn nodded. "That would work."

"Let's include mending skills, while we're at it." Opal clucked her tongue. "Do kids these days know how to sew on buttons?"

"Good idea," Naomi agreed. "Teens could earn coupons at local stores exchangeable for clothing or sewing supplies to make their clothes. Either way, they'd learn sewing basics and contribute to others in need."

"This is great!" Liz's last reservation disappeared. She turned to the window and watched her gardener finish and head for the potting shed to clean up. "Kiera will join us in a minute. Should we sit on this until our next meeting? Or bounce it off her now?"

"Why wait?" Sadie, who had been uncharacteristically quiet, burst into the conversation. "If only somebody had started something like this when I was a farm girl with two dresses to my name." Her blue eyes sparkled. "Let's do it!"

"Liz, you should approach her." Mary Ann had taken the reins once more. But Naomi nodded, and Liz agreed. After all, Kiera knew her best.

But how? As she trimmed seams—keeping a vigilant eye on their width—Liz pondered an opening line. After raising Steve, she'd learned how to approach teen guys. But girls? *Hmm.*

When Kiera walked in, they all looked up to greet her and then returned to their projects.

Good. Kiera usually preferred to stay in the background. Liz handed the girl patterns and material and spread out her own print fabrics alongside Kiera's. Amid pinning and measuring, she told the teen about the quilting project they were considering, with no personal reference to her. "The Material Girls want to raffle it off to benefit a fund that will provide kids with school clothes. Would you like to take part?"

"Yeah!"

If only Kiera knew how her rare smiles changed her entire look. Liz said gently, "When the fund is up and running, we hope to offer teen helpers the opportunity to earn coupons good for clothing in local stores, or for sewing supplies."

"You—you mean that between now and school starting I could earn some new clothes?"

When Liz nodded, the girl's large green eyes moistened. She blinked rapidly as Liz leaned over and pinned a pattern, studiously avoiding Kiera's emotion and trying to hide her own.

Later, when the girl was occupied cutting her own pieces, Liz raised her fist in a mini-pump, and the others met her elation with a chorus of smiles.

After tough adventures in Lafayette and Chicago, she'd come to this Material Girls session hoping it would lift her spirits.

Thanks to her generous friends and their grateful helper, her day had brightened, and her foggy mind had cleared.

Surely, she'd sleep better tonight. Tomorrow, she'd gather her thoughts and plan her next steps.

Gather her thoughts? *Ha!*

Liz's first guests of the weekend, Dale and Lena Carothers, arrived two hours early. They also brought their Yorkshire terrier, a handful of beribboned, big-eyed brown fluff that adored Beans on sight.

The feeling was not mutual. When the yappy little creature circled the bulldog twice with wagging tail, Beans did not condescend to open his eyes. But Liz, who now interpreted his moods almost as well as Sadie, saw his left ear quiver and then his right—Beans's "strike one."

"Isn't that cute?" Lena, a big-haired, fifty-something woman wearing sparkly designer jeans, pursed full magenta lips. "Angel Baby has found herself a playmate."

Angel Baby? "Maybe she'd like to run in the yard," Liz suggested. "I could keep an eye on her while you get settled." Not that she needed more to do, but Beans had opened both eyes—strike two—and she'd much rather dog-sit than referee a dogfight in her foyer.

"Take her new boyfriend with you." Lena blew a kiss to the Yorkie as she headed up the stairs. "I wouldn't want my Angel Baby to be lonely."

Liz merely answered with a smile, edging the little dog away from Beans. When Lena disappeared, Liz grabbed Angel Baby and hurried out the front door.

I should have asked for her leash. The Yorkie ran back and forth in the front yard like a frantic toddler. Liz dashed after her, grabbing, diving, and missing her. Angel Baby yipped and ducked, apparently overjoyed to have a playmate.

Me? Not so much. Liz needed to catch the little escapee, hopefully before she keeled over and grass-stained every inch of her white capris.

"Need help?" Sarah stood at the top of the steps, looking cool and calm, even in a long-sleeved dress.

"Please." Liz tried not to wheeze.

Sarah moved faster than Liz had imagined. They had almost cornered the dog when a horse pulling a wagon *clip-clopped* down the street. To Liz's horror, Angel Baby made a mad dash straight toward the huge animal's front hooves.

Sarah dove from one side, and Liz from the other. A person flashed from nowhere, lunging full length between them, capturing the Yorkie as they all crashed together in the grass past the sidewalk.

Liz didn't want to move.

Could she move?

The others were untangling legs and arms, so she figured she'd better try.

Her limbs did not cooperate.

"Are you ladies all right?" a deep masculine voice asked.

She looked up into the eyes of Jackson Cross. "I'm just ducky." Panic gripped her. "Where's Angel Baby?"

"Angel Baby?" His expression said, *Did you suffer a concussion?*

The wagon's driver, an old farmer, had hopped down, leathery face full of concern. He spoke in heavily accented English. "You are okay, ja?"

Sarah, cheeks flushed red as apples, had already stood. Jackson handed her the Yorkie, who barked as if the pileup were their fault.

Jackson extended a hand to Liz. "Do you think you broke something? Maybe I should take you to the emergency room."

"No way." Liz struggled to her feet, trying to sweep her hair from her face. "I already have two guests, with more arriving soon." She waved the elderly man back to his wagon. "I'm so sorry this happened. I'm fine, really."

After receiving more assurances, the driver finally left.

"Do you need my help?" Sarah offered her free arm. The Amish girl's dress had suffered no damage, her Kapp had remained on her unmussed hair, and Liz guessed her own bruises from today's adventure would outnumber Sarah's ten to one.

"No, thanks. I'm fine." She turned to Jackson, mortification boiling through her veins. "I-I really appreciate your help in catching Angel Baby. If you hadn't come along—"

"Glad to help." He still wore a quizzical expression. "Is she your dog?"

No, thank goodness. "She belongs to my guests, Mr. and Mrs. Carothers."

"Oh." He brushed off his jeans and glanced at his watch. "Whoa. Well, I'd better hightail it to my meeting."

"Thanks again," she offered lamely as he strode away.

Jackson's hair appeared intact as well. He would arrive at his meeting looking handsome and professional, even in jeans.

Liz surveyed her own torn, green-splotched capris, askew top, and dirty knees and hands. As for her hair—dare she look in a mirror?

"There you are." Lena Carothers, hurrying from the steps, infused a tiny note of reproach in her voice. "Dale and I can't wait to explore downtown, and we want to take Angel Baby with us. Unless you can't bear to give her up."

Liz summoned a wide, false smile. "No, I'm sure she's been missing you."

Lena took the Yorkie in her arms and meandered back to the inn, murmuring, "Poor widdle girl, she's been missing her mama."

Sarah made a choking sound. When Liz glanced her way, though, she saw Sarah hide a grin behind her hand, the first she'd seen on the girl's face since Isaac's arrest.

Seeing that smile, Liz decided the whole doggone episode was worth it.

The Morgans' arrival that evening actually lessened Liz's work, rather than increasing it. Debbie Morgan possessed the gift of getting along with everyone, including Lena. Debbie also had owned Yorkies. She adored Angel Baby sufficiently to seal Lena's friendship for life. Merrill Morgan and Dale also clicked, so the couples explored Pleasant Creek and surrounding areas together, not even returning for coffee hour. Both Liz and Beans greatly appreciated the Yorkie's accompanying them. The other couple who arrived Friday evening required little attention as well. Liz even had time to scan and email the mystery note to a translation service. She enjoyed her guests and the uncomplicated weekend. They all left after Sunday breakfast, having complimented her profusely.

"Angel Baby wants to come back too." Lena waved the dog's paw at Liz as they drove away.

I won't tell Beans.

Liz went to church, welcoming the pastor's encouraging message that recharged her spiritual batteries. After cleaning the inn's kitchen and stripping beds, she swam, read, and rested, preparing herself to travel to Countryside Commons the next day.

After poking around scary buildings in Chicago, nosing around new luxury homes sounded nice . . . if the scary people hadn't moved there.

16

West Appleton Avenue, which sounded a little like a street in a children's book, had proved more sinister than Liz cared to remember. But Countryside Commons, with a similar friendly moniker, looked even *better* than it sounded. Located not far from Fort Wayne, with interstate access, it remained separated from congestion and noise by forests and fields. A nearby small town, Staffordsville, added to its charm and practicality.

Liz parked in a cul-de-sac surrounded by two lots with "sold" signs and a large two-story house. Styled to appear old-fashioned, its gables, small white pillars, and stained glass entry bespoke exceptional craftsmanship. Wandering through the subdivision, she saw more "sold" lots and several houses in progress.

Amish workers. Liz tried not to stare at the many straw-hatted, bearded men smoothing concrete and hammering nails. She assumed a "just checking out the neighborhood" air, sending occasional glances the workers' way.

No Simeon Graber—so far.

How about the others? Had she seen any at the barn raising? Or when she was driving around Pleasant Creek's downtown? Liz smothered a sigh of frustration. Besides gray beards and height differences, few distinguishing characteristics helped tell them apart. Their uniform blue shirts and black pants were designed to keep individuals from standing out. Liz lingered as long as she dared and then continued through the subdivision.

Each new home had been landscaped with care, and several included fairly elaborate patios. At the model home at the entrance, a receptionist greeted her. The house featured handmade cabinets, hardwood floors, and spacious bathrooms. Running her hand over lovely woodwork, Liz surmised that people who lived in Countryside Commons obviously did well for themselves.

From what she had seen, sales had been brisk. She mentally scrolled through the prices she'd viewed on Countryside Commons' website. Though a little low for these exceptional homes, surely, they didn't ruin Clarence Peabody.

Some other factor must have entered into his financial misfortune.

Liz headed for Staffordsville, the county seat. The courthouse, located in the middle of the town square, reassured her. Hopefully, she'd glean tidbits of extra information here that would steer her investigation in the right direction.

"Good morning." The elderly secretary in the records office smiled.

She sounds as if she really thinks it's a good morning. "Hello." Liz returned the friendly tone. "I've been looking at houses and thought I'd check a few records." She broadened her smile. "If you know any extra details about the area, I'd love to hear them."

The woman's eyes sparkled. "I've lived here all my life and wouldn't live anyplace else."

Ye-e-ss! Exactly the kind of person Liz had hoped to encounter. The empty office offered the possibility of a fact-mining conversation. The woman hauled out large books of real estate and building records. Liz sat in a hard, clunky chair remarkably like those in the Pleasant Creek courthouse. Deciphering the inky, sometimes unclear handwritten lists took time, especially since she didn't know exact dates of purchase of land or homes. But with the secretary's help, she found several of the houses she'd seen that morning.

"The prices they're asking are out of my range," she told the woman, "but I loved the houses there."

The secretary echoed her enthusiasm. "Those Amish workers created something lovely out of a problem."

"Problem?" Liz tried not to sound too eager.

"Yes." The woman clucked her tongue. "Such a shame. I knew the man who used to own the foundry located there, years ago."

A foundry. Liz's mind circled the word.

"Uncle Joe was such a nice man." The woman's crisp tones faded as she traveled to the past. "He wasn't really my uncle. Joe Butler was his name. But all of us kids called him Uncle Joe. He played baseball with us and sneaked us candy at church."

"He sounds like a wonderful person." Liz curbed her impatience, though her pulse raced.

"He was." She sighed. "Uncle Joe and his family owned the foundry for decades. They had no idea that in 'protecting' their employees with asbestos, they were hurting them and contaminating the area. They dumped chemicals too, not realizing they were poisoning the land and water. None of us understood those things then."

Liz's pulse sped to a gallop. "When did they find out?"

"Not for a long time." The secretary shook her head. "After Uncle Joe died, the foundry went downhill during a recession. His family couldn't find a buyer. It sat idle until a few years ago, when the Amish builders bought it and the surrounding land."

"Even though it was contaminated?" Liz leaned forward.

"They didn't know, at first. Nobody knew." Her face brightened. "The mayor, the town council—the whole town was so excited when they bought the old foundry. Besides being downright dangerous, it had become an eyesore. It's a shame, though, that the builders didn't realize they had to clean up the contamination."

"Do you happen to remember any names? I might want to talk to them about a house."

"I can look them up." The woman leafed through a large brown book, chuckling. "Sometimes I see their work crews at the café here on the square. Those men can really eat! Phyllis Anderson, who owns it, says she has to reorder whenever they show up."

"I've been at a barn raising." Liz kept her voice casual,

though she wanted to grab the book herself. "They eat tons."

"Here we are." The secretary pointed. "Meister Builders."

Not Midwest Services? Liz wilted. "Are they out of Chicago?"

"No, it says here they're from Indianapolis."

Okay. Liz extended her hands. "May I see?"

"Certainly." The secretary handed Liz the heavy volume and left to answer a ringing phone.

She studied the blotted entry. Yes, Meister Builders had applied for a permit and Richard Clayton—whoever he was—was listed as the owner. She inhaled sharply. His representative, Simeon Graber, had signed the application!

At last! Liz fell back, bumping the back of her head on the uncompromising chair. But she didn't care. She'd found something concrete to confirm the connection between Simeon and Countryside Commons! She took pictures with her phone.

The secretary bustled in. "I hate to interrupt you, but I'll be leaving for lunch in a few minutes."

"I'm sorry." Liz glanced at the plain-faced wall clock. "I didn't realize it was noon."

"No problem." The woman grasped the weighty book Liz handed her. "Did you find what you were looking for, Ms., er—?"

"Byler." Liz hated to lie, but what if someone tried to track her actions? "Yes, I did. Thanks for your help."

"That's what I'm here for. If you need to come back after one, feel free." The secretary beamed as she walked Liz to the entrance. "After Meister Builders cleaned up that mess, they went ahead with the subdivision. Countryside Commons has been wonderful for our town. Makes other people want to move here. And though the homeowners generally work in the city, they also participate in our community. A win-win for everybody, don't you think?"

"Absolutely. Thanks again." Liz smiled and left for the café on the town square, her mind spinning.

Meister Builders had paid to decontaminate the land? Yet, at the barn raising, it was implied that the girls' boyfriends and husbands—and presumably, Simeon—had made excellent profits. How could that be if the company had been forced to unexpectedly spend thousands upon thousands to remove asbestos and chemicals?

Clarence had included Countryside Commons on his website as one of his projects, but where and when did Peabody Construction enter this picture?

When she walked into the café, an apple-shaped, sixtyish server told Liz to sit and make herself at home. The restaurant's 1970s dark paneling and flocked wallpaper ordinarily would have bugged her, but what she'd learned at the records office trumped even green-and-gold fuzzy wallpaper.

She dropped into a booth and ordered a hamburger because she didn't want to bother with a menu. As she stirred her excellent coffee, Liz pondered the details she'd discovered. *You'll find answers, Liz,* she admonished herself. *Think.*

The idea that Meister Builders had conned Peabody into responsibility for the cleanup sounded bizarre. However, if that was somehow true, the records secretary was right. It was a win-win situation for that company, for Simeon, and for Staffordsville.

Just not for Clarence Peabody.

Her thoughts returned to her lunch with Gene. He'd said his brother had been mesmerized by an Amish man, Abe Brenneman, who headed Midwest Services, a company that apparently no longer existed. Gene thought Brenneman had talked his brother into a scheme that bankrupted his business.

Was it a scheme in which Clarence had had to clean up contaminated land?

Gene claimed he had conducted their partnership's business dealings. Without his brother's guidance, Liz reasoned, Clarence might have proven easy pickings for a corrupt front man with an honest face.

An honest face.

Liz dropped her spoon. What if Abe Brenneman and Simeon Graber were one and the same?

Were Midwest Services and Meister Builders also connected? How?

"Would you like me to reheat your burger?"

Liz blinked.

The waitress eyed her and then her enormous sandwich with an incredulous grin. "Unless, of course, you like 'em stone cold."

Liz summoned a small chuckle. "Actually, no. I was just thinking—"

"Too much on your mind, right?" The server shook her head. "We all do it, instead of enjoying our food, the way God intended. I'll be glad to fix that."

Are you Mary Ann's sister? Nevertheless, Liz nodded, and her self-appointed life coach disappeared, returning moments later with the steaming hamburger, lettuce and tomato still cool and crisp. Liz's mouth watered. The big bite she took apparently satisfied the waitress, who hurried off to share more helpful advice.

Liz munched away, weighing her latest musings. Gene had seen Abe Brenneman, Midwest's representative, but only a couple of times. If she sent him a photo of Simeon Graber, would Gene recognize him as Abe? Would he even open an email from her, after their less-than-friendly parting?

Then there was the problem of obtaining a photo.

She tried to imagine walking up to the respected Amish community leader: "Hi, Simeon. Smile while I take your picture."

Right.

A local newspaper story or perhaps an article in a construction trade magazine might provide one, as Simeon was well known. But even this seemed unlikely. The Amish avoided photos of themselves, thinking them prideful, even violations of the Second Commandment, which prohibited making "graven images."

Maybe one of the Material Girls had taken his picture during a town celebration or gathering. What excuse could she give Mary Ann to track one down for her?

She also needed to find evidence Clarence Peabody had been involved in Meister's original purchase of Countryside Commons land. If only she could find something today. So far, she'd seen only the records of Meister Builders' sales to present home and lot owners. Estimating time needed for a major ecological cleanup, Liz guessed the original foundry purchase must have taken place at least two years earlier. Back to the dusty real estate books. She sighed. *What I wouldn't give for a nice searchable computer database!*

Still, if today she could find written evidence of Peabody's dealings with Meister Builders, she would've discovered concrete support for their involvement in his ruin. Had Clarence been planning to expose them? If so, that seemed the perfect motive for murdering him.

At least, she thought so. Would the police agree?

After finishing her meal, Liz noted all her facts and ponderings in her phone.

Her waitress, directing an approving glance at Liz's empty plate, zoomed by, juggling several others. "Bring you more coffee in a sec."

How does she move so fast? The woman's nametag read Phyllis. Perhaps she was the café's owner, which explained why she treated the place as her personal domain.

Now that Liz was in Phyllis's good graces, maybe she could coax additional information from her. Had Peabody eaten here?

Her glance found Phyllis again, cheerfully bullying a group of men into eating their vegetables. Even more than the records secretary, this woman probably kept her fingers on the town's pulse. When Phyllis zipped back, Liz, in order to sweeten her time with her, ordered lemon pie.

"That's what I like to see." Phyllis warmed her coffee. "Girls who actually eat. Too many skinny women around today."

After this, I won't be one of them. Still, Liz said, "This is wonderful."

She wasn't flattering anyone. The tart-sweet pastry with its thick mantle of meringue rivaled Mary Ann's.

"If everybody would just toss all that tofu and kale stuff into the garbage where it belongs, this world would be a lot less grouchy."

A small bell dinged in Liz's head. "Have you ever served any really grumpy customers?"

The owner chuckled, a low whiskey laugh that shook her stomach under her apron. "Plenty. We all got problems. But a good dinner and good service usually takes care of that."

Liz opened her eyes wide. "But people have left here still cranky?"

Phyllis scrunched her eyebrows. "Only a couple in the thirty-plus years I've owned this place. 'Course, folks who have been at a funeral don't smile, but that's not being grouchy. Grouchy is when you're out to kill everybody, probably for a reason that isn't nearly as justifiable as you think it is."

"I'm sure you're right."

"Of course I am." She rubbed her chin. "One fella, ten years ago, might have been kind of borderline. Somebody without insurance had totaled his brand-new car and sent him to the emergency room. But the other one, a few years back—now he was *grouchy,* no doubt about it."

Quieting her inner yammering, Liz sipped her coffee. "What do you think was bothering him?"

"Don't know." Phyllis grabbed a cup from a nearby multilayered stack and poured coffee for herself. "Out-of-town fella. Seemed okay the first few times I saw him. Even happy. But one day he threw a fit, saying his meat wasn't done." She rolled her eyes. "We cooked it twice, practically turned it into charcoal, but he grumbled the rest of the meal. After he finally left, I figured we'd seen the last of him. 'Good riddance,' I told Charlie—that's the cook—but nooo." She gulped coffee like a shot.

"He came back?"

"Did he ever. I have never, ever taken care of such a nasty customer in my life. He got worse every time. Food never pleased him. Sometimes, he left half of it on his plate. Snarled at everybody like they were dirt, and never left more than a quarter tip. A *quarter*!" Her friendly face purpled. "He even called me fat and said I talked too much."

Clarence Peabody. Liz inserted proper indignation into her voice. "The nerve of him! Was he just young and didn't know better?"

"I could have excused his rudeness, maybe, if he had been." Her wrath flamed up again. "But he was my age or older. Maybe if he'd eaten more, he would have acted like a human being."

"One of those skinny people?" Liz ventured.

"Oh, yeah. Scrawny, with a really bad haircut." Phyllis exhaled noisily. "I'd never thrown anybody out in my life, not even those who'd had a little too much to drink. But that guy—I finally told him to leave and never come back."

It had to be Peabody. Quickly, Liz summoned a newspaper article about his murder on her phone and enlarged his photo to fill the screen. "By any chance was it this guy?"

"Lordamercy, yes, that's him! He was in the paper?" Phyllis's eyes widened, then she guffawed. "Probably wasn't elected mayor, was he? Somebody must have shot him."

Before Liz had to answer, another customer gestured to Phyllis, so she bustled off.

You're more right than you know. Elation won over sadness, though, as Liz typed in her new information, paid the teenage girl at the old-fashioned cash register, and waved goodbye to Phyllis, who told her to be careful going home.

Back to the courthouse records. She would search until she found the foundry's original purchase. Afterward, she hoped to wander Countryside Commons again.

Simeon, I hope you're working there. Be ready to smile and say "cheese."

"Eureka!"

Liz spoke only to herself, as the courthouse secretary had returned to her post. Her finger pointed to the foundry purchase a few years earlier, by Peabody Construction and Midwest Services.

The implications sucked away her breath. Had Midwest Services and Abe/Simeon really conned Clarence into co-signing for the purchase and then disappeared, leaving him responsible for payments and cleanup? That certainly would have bankrupted him, then infuriated him if he'd discovered Midwest Services—born again as Meister Builders—had bought his foreclosed land and was now developing it at an excellent profit.

The sun was sprinting toward the west. She'd better hurry if she wanted to attempt a photo of Simeon today. Before leaving the courthouse, Liz stopped in the restroom to hurriedly pin up her hair and don sunglasses. A small change, but enough, she hoped, to disguise the fact this was her second trip to the subdivision.

Liz drove east and parked in a school bus turnaround a few hundred yards from the Countryside Commons entrance. She wandered past houses, taking occasional photos as if interested in real estate.

Good, the construction crews are still working. She ventured into the yard of an empty house next to another where a group labored. Aiming her phone at the completed house, she took pictures from varied angles. Several Amish men stared, but apparently convinced she was interested in the home, they remained focused on their project.

Liz swept sideways glances at the crew. No Simeon. Still,

she managed to include workers in her pictures' backgrounds. Irrelevant research sometimes morphed into relevant. She had no luck in her other photographic forays either. Maybe he was working elsewhere today.

Perhaps Simeon was conducting more than one con? She shivered. Could he really be that corrupt?

Don't get carried away, Liz. She hadn't yet proved his involvement in the Midwest and Meister situation; right now it was little more than guesswork. She also wanted to check out Richard Clayton, the owner of Meister Builders.

She stopped at the model home again, affirming her house-hunting persona, just before it closed.

Sweaty after her walk back, she welcomed her car's cool interior as she wearily drove toward the interstate. She'd made progress, but until Simeon/Abe's identity and involvement in both transactions was established, informing the police of her suspicions wasn't an option.

At least I'm not going on hunches and gut reactions alone now.

City traffic had subsided, and she basked in the ease of cruise-control driving until a big-fendered pickup pulled into the passing lane, its bright lights bouncing off her mirrors. Liz hated changing them, so she slid slightly to one side in her seat to compensate for the glare. The truck sped up, but remained behind her, dazzling her vision to the point of near blindness.

What's your problem? Pass me! Liz removed her foot from the gas pedal.

The pickup slowed too.

Gripping the steering wheel, she pressed the accelerator again.

Her unwanted companion sped up.

Liz's breath caught in her chest. Fixing aching eyes ahead, she forced herself to breathe. To think. Maybe this guy just didn't like women drivers. Maybe he thought it was cute to scare them.

Or maybe he didn't like her closing in on information that was supposed to stay buried.

Her fuel gauge read just below full. She didn't know the area, other than the interstate, so she'd be no match for someone who did. Liz bent over the wheel, gritting her teeth. "Think you can outrun me? We'll see."

She floored it.

The truck roared close behind, like a lion with open jaws. For sparsely populated miles, it pursued, playing with her Acura as if it were prey. Liz blinked repeatedly in an effort to offset the awful glare.

Can't see him. Her? Them?

Given her distorted vision, she refused to push too fast, but she kept her speed well above eighty, hoping a police car would chase them.

C'mon, I want a ticket!

No such luck.

Finally she saw a sign for a state police station three exits away. She'd pull off there and dare this creep to follow.

Instead, he took the next exit.

Something in her wished she could follow him to the stoplight, jump out of her car, and smash his windows with a tire iron.

But I'd have to get the tire iron out of the trunk first. So she probably should go with Plan B: Stop at the police station and tell her story. Or Plan C: Chalk up the pursuit as the action of an idiot and go home.

She couldn't prove he'd harassed her. Even if the police caught the guy, he could make *her* look like the idiot, a paranoid woman who shouldn't be driving alone at night.

Maybe she was paranoid. Had she let her imagination get the best of her?

Forcing her rubbery arms and legs to continue, Liz went with Plan C.

Not even the prospect of a lakeside rendezvous with the moon tempted her to her bench. She reached the inn, wobbled into her room, and fell onto her bed, her mind spinning with conspiracy theories and what-ifs even as she surrendered to a deep slumber.

17

"Why do you want a picture of Simeon Graber?" Mary Ann cocked her head as she spoke, halting her needle in the middle of embroidering a quilt block.

Liz fiddled with pins. Though they were alone in Sew Welcome's workroom—Sadie had gone to lunch with a friend—she couldn't help glancing around. How had she convinced herself Mary Ann wouldn't ask questions? Liz fidgeted as if she was six again, facing her school principal. "I-I can't really tell you, at this point. I don't have enough evidence to support what I'm thinking."

Mary Ann's gaze drilled into her. "But you have some evidence, correct?"

"Some." Liz waited while Mary Ann weighed her next words.

No photos of Simeon had shown up on the Internet. Liz had ransacked the library, as well as the local historical society, as best she could. She couldn't afford to ask the librarian or any other locals for help.

No one but Mary Ann.

Trying to re-pin a pattern, Liz stuck one under her fingernail. "Ouch!"

No sympathy was forthcoming from Mary Ann. She said, "Simeon is a prominent man in this part of the state, and not only among the Amish. I've been a family friend for years, you know."

"I don't want to make trouble." How Liz wished Mary Ann would blink. "If my hunch doesn't pan out, I promise I will never breathe a word to anyone. It will die with me." Liz swerved her gaze to meet her friend's.

Mary Ann, arms crossed, tapped her forefingers on her elbows. "I believe you."

Liz felt almost as rubbery as after her encounter with the psycho pickup. "Thank you."

"Sadie takes pictures everywhere. She gives me copies for my History of Pleasant Creek albums."

Why am I not surprised?

"She took several at Simeon's daughter's wedding several years ago. Did it on the sly, of course. I'm sure he's in at least one." Mary Ann nodded, as if answering inner questions. "I'll scan one and email it to you tonight."

"I hope it will clarify some issues." Despite her appreciation, Liz's mind scrolled through the inn's to-do list, hoping to escape this uncomfortable conversation.

"Speaking of pictures," Mary Ann said casually, "the photo of that young woman you had on your living room mantel was lovely."

I should have known. Tit for tat. Liz blurted, "It is pretty, isn't it?"

Again, Mary Ann glued her gaze to Liz's. "The girl resembles a friend who worked with me in my mother's sewing shop, back when we were teenagers. Her name was Deborah Miller. We've lost track of each other, so I wondered if you happened to know her."

Why did the name sound familiar? Liz chewed her lip. In her research, had she run across it? Nevertheless, she could look Mary Ann in the eye and say, "No, I've never met a Deborah Miller."

"A shame. We were good friends, and I'd love to catch up." Mary Ann returned to her quilting block.

Liz put away her work and rose to leave. "Thanks again for agreeing to send me Simeon's picture. I hope I'm wrong about him." Despite her eagerness to help Isaac and Miriam, Liz meant it.

Mary Ann gave her another searching look. "I hope you are too."

On her tablet's screen, Liz studied the photo of Simeon, wearing a black suit, sitting by his daughter on her special day. Simeon's hair had grayed since it was taken, but he was definitely recognizable. At the carefully veiled happiness in his eyes, Liz cringed. She cropped the beaming bride out of the picture and edited the photo, her gut tightening by the moment.

If she was right about Simeon, she would destroy his whole world.

But Clarence Peabody's world had been destroyed. As was Isaac's and Miriam's and Sarah's if the real perpetrator wasn't found.

If Simeon was guilty, she couldn't stand by and watch him devastate other lives.

Perhaps even hers.

Liz saved Simeon's cropped photo to her computer and opened an email to Gene. What could she say that would move him? Finally, she typed:

Dear Gene,

I understand your hesitation to allow me access to Clarence's business records, but I believe I may have found the man who talked him into the contract that sank his company. I've attached his photo. If this is Abe Brenneman, your identification would bring us one step closer to true justice for Clarence, as well as for others. But if you cannot positively identify him—I know you saw him only a couple of times—please say so. Thanks for your consideration.

Sincerely,

Liz Eckardt

She read and reread the email and then attached a silent prayer, along with the photo, before hitting "send."

She didn't expect an immediate reply. Gene might not even bother to read it. She rechecked Midwest Services' site, still on the Web—neither Richard Clayton nor any other staff were cited there.

So she conducted a search for Clayton, whom she thought might be the head of the phantom company. As Liz expected, dozens of Richard Claytons popped up on her screen, connected with all kinds of companies. She focused on construction and real estate businesses scattered throughout the Midwest, finding nothing that overtly tied those Richard Claytons to Simeon or Countryside Commons.

Nothing seemed to click or connect. A small ache in her shoulders had burgeoned into full-fledged pain, and her eyes felt sandpapery. Liz debated with herself whether to check email before she turned in. *Even if Gene bothered to open your email, he would never answer this fast. So why disappoint yourself?*

She checked anyway.

No answer from Gene appeared. But the translation service had sent the English version of the anonymous note she'd received. Liz's yawn halted halfway. *The language is a Swiss-German Amish dialect*, the email read. *We have translated it as follows: "Your wickedness will punish you. Your backsliding will rebuke you. Consider then and realize how evil and bitter it is for you when you forsake the Lord your God and have no awe of me," declares the Lord, the Lord Almighty.*

Not exactly a comforting devotional before bedtime. Liz searched a Bible website and confirmed it as a scripture, Jeremiah 2:19. Did the note assert Simeon's hostility toward her—or that of Philip, Miriam's husband?

One thing was clear: Someone disliked her, or possibly her investigations, enough to send the note.

What if that resentment took a more violent turn?

Should she call Chief Houghton? Or was she overreacting to a harmless effort to discourage her presence in Pleasant Creek?

Liz first rechecked the dead bolts on the inn's front door and then that of her bedroom. She wrapped her mother's quilt around her and went to bed.

I won't go to the police yet. She'd wait at least until she'd heard from Gene.

But for the first time since moving to Pleasant Creek, a security system seemed like a good idea.

Liz entered the Pleasant Creek library and ascended the stairs, anticipation speeding her steps. Glancing around the near-empty fiction area, she spotted Miriam sitting at a table and slid into a chair beside her. "How are you?"

Miriam's wan face squeezed Liz's heart. "I am hopeful."

You don't sound hopeful. Liz clasped her hand, and they joined silences for a moment.

What to say next? Liz ventured, "I was surprised when you called. I didn't even know you had a phone."

"Philip keeps one in the barn for business and emergencies."

He probably doesn't consider this an emergency. But we do.

"I hope you don't mind meeting me here," Miriam continued. "He asked me not to shop at Sew Welcome for a while."

Because their quilts are a bad influence, right?

Miriam looked down at her hands. "Though he's gone right now, his family is not."

Liz kept her face calm, but in her lap her hands clenched into fists.

"Philip is a good man," Miriam said gently. "In his way, he is trying to protect me."

Liz wanted to say, "I understand," but she didn't, so she asked, "How is Isaac?"

Surely Miriam couldn't bear to stay away from her son forever. With one look at the brief gleam in her friend's eye, Liz knew.

Shunning or no shunning, Miriam had seen the boy.

"He says the food at the jail tastes like mud." The Amish woman chuckled, though it sounded more like a sob. "He tried to make me leave because he feared the consequences of my coming. But I know he was glad to see me."

"I'm sure he was."

Silence again. But Liz sensed an easing of Miriam's heaviness just with the few words they shared. How hard not to mention your child's name to family and friends, though grief and pain swelled inside you like a raging infection! "How did you manage to see him? When?"

Miriam's full pink mouth firmed into a thin line. "Yesterday Simeon Graber asked Philip and the boys to help raise a house and barn near Hayworth. After they left, my girls went to stay with their cousins." She raised her chin. "I waited until dusk and walked to town to see Isaac."

Liz ached to tell Miriam that perhaps, indeed, there was reason to hope for her son's release. But she couldn't do that yet. If only Gene would answer her email . . . "I've been praying for you and your family every day."

"Please don't stop." Miriam dabbed at her tears, then she said firmly, "Let's talk about something different, something positive."

Liz regaled her with descriptions of the Meisner wedding, the shivaree, and adventures with Angel Baby. She'd never heard Miriam giggle before. In that instant, she wished they could have grown up together, sharing secrets in the haymow, taking walks on starry nights.

Finally, Miriam quieted and straightened her Kapp. "I must go to my sister's and pick up Grace and Keturah."

She sounded like a soccer mom.

Liz smiled. "I'm sure they had fun."

"Probably too much." Miriam smiled. "The last time they stayed there, they raced carts until the poor ponies were worn out. But it was good for Grace and Keturah to get away." She hugged Liz once more. "Thank you for your friendship. For your prayers."

Liz watched Miriam's blue-clad, black-capped figure disappear down the stairs. Then, for the sixth time that morning, she checked email on her phone.

Her jaw dropped.

A reply from Gene.

It contained four words: "Yes. That's Abe Brenneman."

So what do I do now?

18

Sometimes guests consumed Liz's time like newborns. Sometimes they cut her some slack.

She raced her thoroughbred vacuum cleaner around the Heirloom room as if competing in a derby, though she didn't need to. This wedding party wouldn't arrive until tomorrow afternoon. Emily, who had made reservations for herself and Jill, one of the Louisville quilters who had been among Liz's first guests, wouldn't arrive until Sunday afternoon.

Liz could take her time preparing for the guests.

Or she could drive to Hayworth where the Amish were helping to build a new house and barn.

And what would she do when she got there? Confront Simeon Graber?

During her efforts to find his photograph, she'd discovered the extent of Simeon's reputation—actually, the family reputation for several generations. Despite their Amish tendency to downplay accomplishments, Simeon, his father, and his grandfather had established patterns of tireless leadership, faithful community service, and openhanded charity, patterns also reflected in Simeon's children's lives.

Did she dare try to topple this Pleasant Creek pillar of virtue?

She realized she'd vacuumed the same spot five times. Liz switched it off. Sneezing as she dumped its container of dirt, she wished she could as easily clean up her messy world.

Go to the police. After all, she did possess some concrete evidence that pointed to Simeon's underhandedness.

But what if Gene had mistaken another Amish man for Simeon?

What if Simeon had signed his name on documents, unwittingly participating in fraudulent real estate schemes hatched by Richard Clayton or some other mastermind?

Even after only six weeks in Pleasant Creek, she realized the power of small-town rumors. Mere hints of dishonesty could wreck Simeon's life and his family's.

And her own.

She hit the "power" button on the vacuum and zoomed down the hall, wishing its noise could drown out her relentless thoughts.

Not only would her reputation and business suffer, but her Amish relatives, if she found them, would want nothing to do with her.

There would be no more stolen moments with Miriam either. Her friend's wounded face floated before her, and the equally wounded faces of Isaac and Sarah.

She remembered her mother's strong, loving face, and her no-compromise voice telling her, "Always tell the truth, Liz. Stand up for the truth. In telling God's truth, we show we are His."

Liz switched off the vacuum and went downstairs to her bedroom where she traded her jeans for a skirt.

What's the hurry? a voice yammered in her ear. *At least, wait until Simeon returns. Give it time. You need to think this through.*

But she'd done enough thinking. Liz jumped into her car for another drive through the peaceful Indiana countryside, feeling as if she were headed for the O.K. Corral at high noon.

Two hours later, she pulled into the town of Hayworth, which consisted of a dozen houses, a post office, and a convenience store/laundromat/computer repair shop. One cup of coffee and a conversation with the friendly clerk gave Liz the location of the house and barn raising. After a couple of righted wrong turns, she parked her car among a sea of buggies in a pasture and walked toward the completed barn and half-finished house. Amish men gathered near tables swarmed by women and children tidying after the noon meal. Liz edged along a cluster of bushes near the scene.

She didn't have trouble locating Simeon. As at the other barn raising, he was conferring with assistants, gesturing to groups of men who followed his calm directions. She waited until the men scattered. Simeon, who apparently had delayed his dessert, accepted chocolate cake from a child and sat at the end of a table.

Liz stepped from her concealment and approached him as he dug in.

"Hello, Abe."

He froze.

The split second did not tell her all.

But the dropped jaw and bulging eyes, as if she'd stabbed him, told her enough.

Before he could resume his Amish reserve, she melted into the bushes and sprinted toward her car.

"Do you know what you're *saying*?" Chief Houghton, bushy eyebrows lowered, sliced into Liz with his razor gaze.

She returned the look. "Yes. And I think something should be done about it."

"I don't think the evidence you've given me is enough to make any charges stick, but I'll check with a few people around the Fort Wayne area and see what comes up." He scribbled notes on a pad. "I also think you should talk to Pleasant Creek's Amish bishop, Nathan Manz."

"The bishop?" Liz stared, but then she recognized the chief's strategy. If she was serious about Simeon's fraud, she would be the one to inform his spiritual leader—not Chief Houghton, who didn't want to harm his good relationship with the Amish community. The bishop would contact Houghton, either to demand the police silence this slanderous English lawyer or to discuss her claims.

Smart. But she'd never even met the bishop.

"However"—the police chief leaned across his cluttered desk on muscular arms, so close his peppermint breath punctuated each syllable—"don't say a word about this to anyone else. Do you understand?"

She didn't budge. "Yes."

His lion look faded to a neutral expression, but his posture didn't relax. "Keep your eyes open, Ms. Eckardt. I don't like that note or that nighttime truck incident on the freeway. Nothing like that happened on your way back from Hayworth, right?"

"No." She didn't tell him she drove fifteen miles an hour over the speed limit.

"Good." Houghton stood, his forehead still furrowed. "Did you happen to keep that note? We can check for fingerprints."

She handed it to him in a folder. "I'm guessing that whoever wrote it, Amish or English, probably knew he should wear gloves."

Trying to look fearless, Liz left. She crossed the street, inhaling drafts of rose-scented evening air. The clock tower loomed before her, its solid presence a comfort, its voice a friend. Eight o'clock. Too late to visit the bishop.

Thank goodness. She'd go tomorrow morning.

As she entered the inn, she almost wished she had more to do. Sarah had taken out her own frustrations on the guest rooms and kitchen. Liz straightened the living room and four-season room, and then made herself do more research on Richard Clayton. She found a few more individuals associated with construction companies and real estate, but, again, no visible connections to Simeon or Countryside Commons surfaced.

Websites could be so deceptive. Midwest Services had certainly proved that. But she couldn't visit all of these companies to confirm their legitimacy. *Even if I call them, I haven't established they exist, or that their Richard Clayton is Meister/Midwest's Richard Clayton.*

I haven't even established that the man exists! Given Midwest's here-one-day-gone-the-next subsistence, Richard Clayton could very well be an alias.

She did stumble, though, on a couple of newspaper articles from cities in Ohio and Kentucky, each of which mentioned Richard Clayton as the head of a different company initiating a new building project.

Liz checked the websites of Housing Advantage in Zanesville, Ohio, and Benefit Building in Paducah, Kentucky. A small alarm buzzed in her mind that increased in volume as she examined their pages. *Shades of Midwest Services.* Like the website of the phantom company that first approached Peabody Construction, both presented excellent building photos and hype about the new projects mentioned in the articles, but very little about the company's history and next to no contact information.

Despite articles citing his name, no one named Richard Clayton could be found on either website. She tried to access the county housing records where the companies were building the new projects, only to find that, like Countryside Commons, they were located just inside nearby rural counties that did not use online records.

Perhaps the reporters who wrote the articles had to examine handwritten records, as Liz had done in Staffordsville, to find out Richard Clayton had participated in the land sales?

Did that land, like the Indiana project, also have a contaminated past, cleaned up by other soon-to-be-bankrupt Clarence Peabodys who hadn't had a clue?

Liz's chest tightened as if she were strapped to the chair.

Facing a police chief today and an irate Amish bishop tomorrow with her suspicions about Simeon Graber had seemed a frightening challenge.

Opposing this Richard Clayton, whose invisible, greedy hands reached across three states, might make those confrontations seem small by comparison.

"You're going to see the bishop?" Mary Ann's eyes widened

over the mug of coffee Liz brought her. Her usual morning sparkle dimmed. "Why?"

"Chief Houghton suggested it."

Her friend's jaw dropped. She whispered, "But Simeon is Bishop Manz's nephew."

Liz's stomach lurched. No wonder Houghton had been reluctant to approach the Amish leader.

Mary Ann turned as if to reenter Sew Welcome. "I'll tell Sadie I'm going with you."

Liz fought the urge to let her. "No. Why should he get mad at you too?" She hurried through the foyer and out the door. Part of her hoped Mary Ann would charge after her in the Sew Welcome van. Another part of her hoped she'd get lost driving to the bishop's house.

For once in her life, Mary Ann paid heed to someone else's instructions. And sadly, Liz didn't make a single wrong turn. A white-haired woman in navy blue answered her knock.

"I would like to see the bishop, please," Liz blurted.

The woman hesitated, then pointed to a straight-backed rocker on the porch. "I'll tell him you're here, Miss—?"

"Eckardt. Liz Eckardt." She tried to fix her mind on the glorious purple irises and orange poppies waving in nearby flower beds, but for once, the beauty of flowers could not soothe her.

No hint of a smile crossed the bishop's face as he let the screen door bang lightly behind him. "What can I do for you, Ms. Eckardt?" He did not sit in the other rocker.

She rose. "I'm sorry to interrupt your morning, but I thought it important to speak with you."

"Regarding?" The white-bearded man wasted no words.

She forced her lips to say it. "Simeon Graber."

Silence. The man, and the very air around him, seemed to turn to stone. Finally, he said, "Go on."

She told him everything. About Gene's identifying Simeon as

Abe Brenneman, the front man for Midwest Services. About the contamination of Countryside Commons, Peabody Construction's forced cleanup and foreclosure, and Simeon's fortuitous reappearance in the prosperous project afterward.

"Clarence Peabody." The bishop's nostrils puckered, as if smelling manure. "He came here one day, ranting and raving about some wrong done to him."

"He was a very unpleasant man," Liz agreed.

"But you're saying you believe Simeon wronged him." The bishop loaded each word with meaning. "That he committed fraud?"

"Yes." *And possibly murder.*

His stone eyes melted into a volcanic glow. "You don't possess much evidence to support your claim."

"Not yet." Liz raised her chin. "But I was hoping you would help uncover the truth."

"Ms. Eckardt, you are making serious accusations." His eyes continued to blaze, though his voice remained calm. "Simeon Graber is a man to whom I would entrust my life, as would many others."

"Yet his actions strongly suggest illegal business activity." She was chipping at steel with a fork, but she couldn't stop. "Ask him about his Abe Brenneman identity—"

"An identity recognized by one man, a man who no doubt dislikes the Amish as much as his brother did." The bishop glared. "Until you can further support your story, Ms. Eckardt, I must ask that you leave. Do not harass Simeon or his family. In fact, do not approach anyone in our community about this or any other issue. They will not answer. Good day."

This time, the man slammed the screen door.

It closed in on Liz—her moments with Miriam, her dream of finding her family. Were they gone forever?

One look at Liz's face, and Mary Ann and Sadie surrounded her with hugs but asked no questions.

"Rest," Mary Ann urged Liz. "Give me your cell phone. We'll answer any calls."

"Go lie down." Sadie gave her a gentle shove toward the living room. "I'll bring you a glass of raspberry tea."

For once, Liz turned up the air-conditioning, not only to combat the humid gray morning, but also so that she could wrap herself in her mother's quilt. After she downed Sadie's tea, the quilt's worn softness seemed to caress her damp cheek and hug Liz in its folds.

When she awoke, her refreshed body coaxed her mind and spirit to finish the day.

She welcomed the wedding party with enthusiasm, shared their stories at coffee hour, and fixed them a rave-inspiring breakfast the next morning. She took photos and showered them with sincere compliments—the bride and groom made a stunning couple, and their attendants matched them like perfect accessories. But their story and her part in it seemed exactly that: a civilized reality show she was watching because she had nothing else to do.

She made preparations for the late brunch she'd serve them the next morning and then grabbed the opportunity to clean her quarters, ignoring the computer that called her to research more about Richard Clayton. Naomi phoned, and they went to a movie, as the wedding party wouldn't show up for coffee hour.

"Have you heard any rumors of a shivaree?" Naomi grinned as they walked back to the inn.

"No, but Mary Ann isn't related to this bride. And I haven't found extra food in my pantry." She eyed her friend. "You wouldn't be part of another shivaree conspiracy, would you?"

"Me?" Naomi asked innocently. "Never."

And so on. And so forth. Liz enjoyed their evening, but every laugh echoed inside her as if she herself had moved out of her body.

Early the next morning, she made seafood quiches and cinnamon rolls. While the rolls were rising, she hurried to the early church service, and the pastor's sermon about Joseph and his years in jail comforted her. God brought Joseph justice, despite his trials.

But if Isaac read the story, would it comfort him? Or his mother?

She brushed away the thoughts as she dashed back to the inn and baked the rolls, sending up clouds of cinnamony fragrance to help rouse her guests and bring them downstairs.

"This is too wonderful," the bride said as Liz brought out quiches, gourmet sausages, and bowls of fresh fruit to dip into a small chocolate fountain.

"Let's stay here forever," the groom teased.

Their accolades warmed Liz, but when they didn't linger, she thankfully cleared up and left the bed linens to be washed the next day. When Emily breezed in, saying Jill's arrival had been delayed until sometime Monday, and then breezed out for the evening, Liz wasn't sorry.

After everyone had left, she took a large box of tissues out to her bench and indulged, for the first time since coming to Pleasant Creek, in a good, long cry. There was no "What did I do wrong?" or "What did I do right?" or "What do I do now?" Tears washed her face and soul like refreshing rain. After a final sob and hiccup, she sat a long while, letting the soft lake breeze dry her face. The late afternoon sun gently warmed it.

A long nap, she decided, *that's what I need.* Then her brain cells might be in working order.

After a glass of lemonade, she went to the rotunda to fetch her quilt, anticipating its loving embrace.

Instead, the quilt lay in a limp heap on the foyer floor, seeming to mourn its own wounds.

Someone had slashed it with a large, ugly *X*.

19

"I know you have to check for fingerprints, but please be careful," Liz pleaded as Chief Houghton placed the quilt in a paper bag. "It was my mother's."

"We'll take every precaution." He sounded reassuring, but his continuous frown said otherwise.

"How will you protect Liz?" Sadie demanded. "Whoever this guy is, he's crazy."

The other Material Girls—minus Mary Ann, whose out-of-town sister had been taken to the hospital—had gathered at the inn when they heard the news. Now clustered around the living room's fireplace, they fixed the chief with a group stare.

"I'll be fine." Liz spoke without conviction. Nevertheless, her friends' concern helped to ease the knots in her stomach.

"You'll be fine"—Sadie set her jaw—"because we won't let you stay here alone."

The chief looked relieved. "I'll send an officer every few hours to make sure you're all right, but I think some company is a good idea."

"Really, I'll be fine." Liz tried not to picture Sadie hovering around her 24/7. "Emily will be here tonight—"

"Who's Emily?" The chief raised his brows.

"Emily Hart, remember? She's stayed here before," Liz answered before Sadie's glower morphed into a rant. "Wait. Emily should know about this." Liz pulled out her cell.

Houghton nodded. "She should."

The librarian, however, seemed more indignant than afraid. "Your mother's quilt? That lovely one in the foyer? I can't believe someone would do that!"

"I can't either," Liz murmured. "I certainly will understand if you cancel—"

"No way. I love the inn. Don't call Jill. I'll check with her, but I'm staying, anyway."

Her lack of fear infused a little courage into Liz. "Emily isn't leaving," she told the group after she hung up.

"But she stays upstairs." Naomi shook her head. "No, I'll camp out on your sofa. We'll sleep with our quilting shears by our sides."

"Nobody in their right mind would mess with a Material Girl holding scissors." Caitlyn struck a tough-woman pose.

"I sure wouldn't." A smile tugged at Chief Houghton's lips, but he said, "Call the station immediately if you notice anything weird around here. I have to go to a training session tomorrow, but Officer Dixon will be glad to help you." He cleared his throat. "Could I speak with you privately for a moment, Liz?"

"Sure." *Now what?* She gestured toward the door to her sitting room, and he followed her through the foyer into her quarters.

"This will only take a second, but Miriam Borkholder wanted you to know." No trace of humor warmed his eyes now. "The department finally received the Peabody reports. Traces of Clarence's blood and DNA were found on Isaac's clothes."

No.

No.

"I'm sorry." His words drifted away into Liz's fog.

Later, she couldn't remember anything else he said. But she did understand his warning to keep this quiet.

He left, taking her quilt with him.

She couldn't call Miriam. Philip was home again. Miriam could not call her.

Liz sank to the floor.

A knock on her door—minutes? hours?—later roused her enough to open it.

Naomi didn't say anything. She simply drew Liz into a hug.

The other Material Girls followed Naomi into the room. Liz didn't bother to hold back tears.

"What a horrible person, to do such a thing to your quilt." Opal's gentleness and faint lilac fragrance couldn't banish the chief's terrible revelation, but they soothed Liz's pain a little.

"A total creep." Caitlyn muttered less generous descriptions under her breath.

"I'm calling Mary Ann." Sadie pulled out her cell.

"No," Liz protested. "Her sister needs her. I have all of you."

In answer, the Material Girls gathered around her in a group hug.

Is this what it feels like to have sisters? Even if she were locked out of the Amish community forever, even if she never found the relatives she craved, Liz had found family.

To her surprise, she felt slightly better the next morning. Liz brewed coffee for herself and Sadie, who had arrived at work an hour early.

"See. I told you no one would bother me." Liz brought Sadie a steaming mug as she unlocked Sew Welcome's door.

"Where's Naomi?" Sadie scanned the foyer as if checking for snipers.

"She got up around four to go to the bakery."

"And you were here alone? With that—that *woman* upstairs?" Sadie double-checked the stairway.

Liz rolled her eyes. "Even in the scariest movies, no chain-saw murderers attack after four a.m. They're sacked out after a busy night."

Sadie *humphed* and pushed her shop door open. It closed with a resounding *thump*.

Dear Sadie. She could make Liz smile without even trying. She sipped her own coffee in the four-season room, watching Kiera diligently weed before the sun turned up its frying-pan heat. As promised, a police car circled the block and cruised slowly past the inn several times—reassuring, yet menacing.

She heard Emily *tap-tapping* down the stairs, so she stood and made her way to the foyer. Her guest looked professional in a light gray suit and heels. "Good morning. Do you want breakfast?"

Emily's eyes lit up. "Do you have any of Naomi's croissants?"

"How about a homemade cinnamon roll and some strawberries?"

"Yum." Emily followed her to the kitchen and, sitting on a stool at the counter, devoured her quick meal. She reapplied her lipstick. "I'm off to Indy. Boring meetings all day long." She frowned at herself in her compact mirror. "I'll be here this evening but not in time for coffee hour."

Liz tried not to show her relief. She didn't feel like playing referee today. "Is Jill still coming?"

Emily grimaced. "I don't know. She says her kid is sick. Tonight will be the soonest she arrives, if she makes it at all. Oh well—I love coming here anyway."

"Have a good day," Liz answered Emily's goodbye as she headed out the back door.

Quiet invaded the kitchen, interrupted only by the dishwasher's hum. Liz thought that a whole day might be enough to recover from the past weekend's wedding guests—and from her disastrous interview with the bishop.

But she was sure it would not be enough to recover from the dark evil that had assaulted her house in broad daylight and violated her mom's quilt. Nor would it be enough to recover from Isaac's despair, or from Miriam's pain—

I can't sink into despondence like this.

Liz remembered how her mother always said hard work could help heal a troubled mind, so she'd do laundry and attack the bathrooms. But after lunch, she'd park on her bench and spend a long, lazy afternoon—the way summer afternoons should be.

Before she began, though, she'd touch base with Kiera, who was still weeding in the backyard. Liz carried her coffee outside, knowing mostly that she just wanted an excuse to sample the brand-new morning air, with its petunia-tinged fragrance.

Kiera stood, her knees encrusted with dirt. "Whoa, what I wouldn't give to look like Ms. Hart." She gestured toward Emily's departing figure. "Such cool clothes, and going off to Chicago."

"Chicago? I thought she was going to Indianapolis."

"Nope." As always, Kiera knew she was right. "She was talking on her phone to some guy—didn't get his name—and said she'd meet him in Chicago this afternoon. She sounded really ticked." The teen grinned.

Maybe I *heard Emily wrong.* Liz briefly discussed Kiera's work week with her and then went inside and threw in the first load of laundry. As she continued through her chores, her mind played with what Kiera had told her. *I could have sworn Emily said she was going to Indy . . . for long, boring meetings.*

Perhaps business had changed Emily's plans. But Liz couldn't quite picture a library emergency. More likely, Emily had a boyfriend in Chicago, and she'd decided to skip her Indy meetings to see him.

Why are you making a big deal about this? Liz turned her attention to the washing and folding of defiant fitted sheets.

Unease rattled in her mind all morning like a tiny pebble in a shoe.

After emptying a pie pan of yesterday's quiche, Liz went outside and flopped onto her bench with her still-unfinished thriller and proceeded to read awhile. But her mind refused to focus.

Finally, Liz slapped the book down and walked to the potting shed which Kiera was to clean and reorganize after lunch. She decided she'd ask the teen about Emily's call again. Perhaps hearing more details might settle her own hyper brain so she could relax.

Approaching the shed, Liz squinted, looking through the open door to see inside the darker space. No Kiera. *She never takes this long a lunch break.*

She stepped through the door. Wait. The teen had said the potting shed was a mess, but flowerpots knocked from a shelf, shattered on the cement floor? Dirt scattered everywhere? The place looked like someone had gotten into a fight.

A fight? *Kiera? Sarah?*

Liz dashed to the house, through the common area, and up the stairs, where she searched until she found her maid cleaning the Heirloom room. "Sarah, have you seen Kiera?"

"No."

The girl sniffed, and her lip curled, as usual. But her gaze readily met Liz's.

Liz saw no evidence that her employees' feud had escalated. Certainly no potting soil smeared Sarah's neat blue dress and white apron.

"Is something wrong?" Sarah searched Liz's face.

"I'm not sure. She's probably talking with Sadie. Or something." Liz charged downstairs to Sew Welcome.

"Sadie, have you seen Kiera?"

"No. Haven't you?" At Liz's reaction, Sadie's eyes flashed a warning like an interstellar robot's. "Did she leave without telling you?"

"Kiera wouldn't do that." Liz punched in the numbers for Kiera's cell phone. A recording told her the call could not be completed. "Payday isn't until next Friday. She's probably run out of minutes."

Still, none of this made sense. No matter what, Kiera wouldn't jeopardize the job she loved and needed.

Liz went to the foyer and rummaged through the desk drawer. "I'll call her mother's work number. Maybe there was some sort of emergency."

But Kiera's mom mostly sounded annoyed when her factory foreman summoned her to the phone. "If that girl's run off, she'll be in trouble when I get home!"

Liz gritted her teeth as she hung up. "So much for maternal instinct."

"I knew she'd react that way." Sadie crossed her arms and then uncrossed them. She placed her hands on Liz's shoulders. "I know you think I'm a crazy old lady—"

"The best crazy quilter in Indiana," Liz finished and couldn't help smiling.

"But something's wrong. We both know it." Sadie gestured toward Liz's desk. "You got Emily's car's license number when she registered, didn't you? Let me call Opal and have her nephew check it out. Check *her* out."

First a murderer. Now a kidnapper? Liz stammered, "Y-you think Emily has something to do with Kiera's absence? Why?"

"I don't know why." Sadie gestured impatiently. "I just *know*."

Liz pondered her choices all of two seconds. First of all, she knew that Sadie would call Opal anyway. Second, Kiera hadn't been gone long enough to be considered a missing person, so there was no point in calling Chief Houghton. Liz bristled as she located her registry in the desk. The girl's mom certainly hadn't acted concerned. But worry was spreading through Liz like storm clouds gathering in a summer sky. Feeling helpless, she showed the number to Sadie and watched her call Opal.

"She'll get ahold of him right away." Sadie stuffed her phone into her pocket like a six-shooter into a holster.

"I suppose—"

"You suppose what?" Sadie eyeballed her again.

"While we're waiting to hear from Opal, I suppose I could call Emily's library in Columbus and, um, make sure she's . . ."

"Legit? Do it."

"Surely Chief Houghton did that when Clarence's body was first discovered," Liz mused. "He considered all of us suspects at that point."

"Do it anyway," Sadie urged.

Eager to do something—anything—Liz searched for the library's website and phoned. She was connected with its employee directory.

Liz wilted. "It's sending me to Emily Hart's extension."

If only Mary Ann had been here to keep Sadie—and her—from jumping to conclusions. Thankful they hadn't yet called the police, Liz waited to hear Emily's voice mail.

Instead, a woman's husky voice answered briskly, "Emily Hart."

She sounded nothing like Emily—the Emily who was supposed to be driving to Chicago. Or was it Indianapolis? Liz choked out, "I-I'm sorry. I must have the wrong number."

The voice's civil tone disappeared. "That blasted directory is malfunctioning again. I've told them again and again to bring back the switchboard operator, but do they listen?"

Still stunned, Liz listened to a rambling tirade against technology and then quickly hung up.

"Emily lied, didn't she?" Sadie's quiet tone jolted Liz almost as much as the phone call.

"Yes." Liz explained the details, hardly believing them herself. "Perhaps there's a logical reason for this. Maybe she's hiding an affair. Maybe she's hiding from an abusive husband."

"She lied because she killed Clarence Peabody." Sadie refused to back down. "And whatever she's done to make Kiera take off, it isn't good."

Liz gulped. "I'd better tell the chief." Pulling out her phone again, she noted the license number Emily—or whoever she was—had given her. "I wish I had a picture of her."

"Didn't you take one for the inn's album?" Sadie gestured to the living room, where Liz kept it on the coffee table.

No. Liz stood stock-still. "She wouldn't let me." There had been more to Emily's laughing refusal than she thought.

"Of course, she didn't let you." Sadie drew out her phone too. "But I caught her in some pictures I took during our quilting party."

The sight of the smiling librarian helping Kiera sew drained away what certainty Liz possessed. How could she be a murderer? And why would she abduct Kiera?

The phone call. Liz's throat closed. Kiera had overheard Emily say she was going to Chicago. Had the girl heard something else—something that made her a target for Emily's wrath?

I have no proof of any of this. I may be imagining the whole scenario. But the chief had told her to report anything unusual. Liz straightened her back. "I'd better go to the police station. What I have to say would sound even weirder over the phone."

"I'm going with you."

"Who'll watch your shop?"

"Opal," Sadie said. "She offered to help. I'll call her again, and Naomi and Caitlyn too. They need to know what's going on."

Liz didn't protest.

She was certain that Kiera needed help, and maybe more help than just the Material Girls could begin to supply.

20

"I wanted to paddle that boy's rear end," Sadie fumed as they left the police station. "He wasn't listening. What a time for the chief to be at a training session. Why didn't he leave someone in charge who knows a thing or two? Or at least shaves!" She slammed the Acura's passenger door so hard the car shook.

Liz would have laughed had she not shared her friend's frustration. "I'm sure Officer Dixon is an excellent policeman. Kiera's mother isn't worried, so why should he be? He did say he'd send a car to her home and check out the usual teen haunts."

"Whoop-de-doo," Sadie sniffed. "Kiera isn't messing around with some boy. She's been kidnapped."

The word slammed Liz in the chest. She said haltingly, "I could tell Dixon thinks Emily is having an affair."

"Is that what you think?" Sadie stuck out her lower lip like a bulldog's.

"No." The figurative pebble rattling in Liz's shoe had grown to a cobblestone. She revved up the car. "First, let's look for Kiera."

"Where?" Sadie leaned forward as if urging on their steed.

Good question. Liz's hand rested on the gear shift. In the empty Midwest Services warehouse in Chicago?

Sadie's cell phone rang. "Hi, Opal. Whatcha got, girl?" she asked.

A small sparkle in her friend's eyes multiplied to diamond proportions. Sadie hung up and pumped her fist. "Ye-e-ss! That woman didn't own that car! She rented it up in Gary."

Rented? "Where's Gary?"

"Near Chicago." Sadie's smile widened every second. "Under the name Jennifer Clayton."

Clayton. As in Richard Clayton. Liz shifted her gears. "You'll have to help me find it, but now I know where we're going. To Simeon Graber's farm."

"Simeon Graber?" Now Sadie turned to Liz, mouth agape. "Have you lost your—?"

"My mind? Maybe." Liz whipped the Acura out of the parking space. "But it's our best bet. I'll tell you why on the way."

A seething Sadie directed Liz down a gravel road that bordered Simeon's property. "If you park there, that grove of trees will hide us from the house and barn."

After hearing Liz's case against Graber, Sadie had called Opal, Naomi, and Caitlyn, giving each of them quick summaries. Naomi had served Kiera and her friends at the bakery several times, so she offered to track down Kiera's friends in case they knew her whereabouts. On speakerphone, Liz gave Caitlyn directions to the Chicago warehouse. Taking her brawny brothers along, Caitlyn would head northwest, hoping to spot Emily's car at a gas station or restaurant by an interstate exit. Sadie and Liz then called Mary Ann and updated her.

"Wait for me," Mary Ann urged. "I'm only a half hour away."

"I wish we could. But if Emily's stowed Kiera here, she probably . . . won't stay long." Liz dared not put her worst fears into words. "We have to find her now. I've got my pepper spray."

"I've got mine too," Sadie yelled into the phone, "but I'd rather punch that lying hussy in the nose."

Half-laughing, half-crying, Liz hung up and swung open her car door. "Let's try the barn first, rather than the house. I don't want to involve Simeon's family until I know something concrete."

Sadie moved faster than most women twenty years younger, easily keeping up with Liz. Maybe her regimen of tangos and farm work kept her in shape. Sadie's gaze shifted from side to side like a flashlight's beam, piercing the darker recesses of the forest. Liz tried to muffle her footsteps as she listened for foreign sounds.

So far, they saw no sign that anyone had been in the vicinity recently. The mossy green woods, with its gentle sighs and whispers, seemed so serene. They crossed a creek, stepping from stone to stone. How could evil lurk in this peaceful place?

Fortunately, the grove of trees extended almost to the cluster of buildings that was coming into view. Liz scanned the landscape, seeing only one Amish worker leaving a barn and walking toward the house. *Everyone must be at dinner.*

Simeon owned two barns, plus numerous outbuildings. Liz frowned. More buildings equaled more hiding places. To save time, she and Sadie would have to split up. "I'll search the bigger barn. You take the smaller one," she whispered.

"I'll check out those two sheds too." Sadie pointed. "And I'll take the corncrib."

"The corn crip?"

"Crib. C-r-i-b. That long building with chicken-wire sides. You search the shed nearest your barn, plus the chicken coop. We can touch base back by the big silos. Let's meet at the one attached to the shed."

"Gotcha." *What if we* don't *find Kiera?* Liz pressed her lips together to keep them from trembling.

Sadie's long, wiry arms embraced her. "Be careful."

Liz hugged her. "Text if you find something."

"You too." Sadie slipped away, stealthy as a spider, toward the side wall of the smaller barn.

Liz waited to ensure that no one had seen her friend and then stole to the side of the long, low chicken coop. Its fenced yard corralled dozens of the softly clucking fowl. Would the whole flock erupt in a cacophony of alarmed cackles if she, a stranger, approached? If so, someone in the house was bound to investigate. Flattening herself against the wall, she tiptoed to the back corner and peered around it.

Seeing no one, she moved to a row of small, open screened windows and peeked inside.

Her stomach lurched at the pungent smell, but she tried to see inside the dusky interior. Hens sat on nests tucked onto parallel shelves. She could see nothing in the narrow space beneath the shelves. A similar venture along the third wall convinced her—as far as she could see—that neither Kiera nor her captor was there.

She sneaked to the door of the enormous white-sided, main barn. She paused a moment to listen. Hearing nothing inside but a whinny or two, she slowly tugged the heavy door open.

No one was in the large aisle between stalls either.

Even as Liz's heart pumped at a furious pace, she noticed the cleanliness of the big room. Mary Ann had said the Amish held church services in their barns.

Church services? In *Simeon's* barn? Bile filled her mouth as she zipped from stall to stall. Big brown horse. No Kiera. Big black horse. No Kiera. No Kiera. No Kiera—

A sound.

It was the front door opening.

Liz skittered to a big, dusty sleigh. She wedged her body between it and the wall.

A deep voice murmured—to a horse?

There were heavy footsteps, walking faster now.

Simeon approached. He had worried eyes, like at the barn raising.

Liz held her breath.

He passed her hiding place and thumped out the back door.

She waited for it to close and then darted forward to the stalls she hadn't yet checked.

There were horses. Only horses.

She dashed to the back door and cracked it open slowly. She watched Simeon's broad-backed, straw-hatted figure as he walked past the sheds and the other large barn.

She texted Sadie: *SG. Going toward silos?*

Sadie texted back: *Looks like it. Following.*

Liz shadowed Simeon, moving swiftly from building to building.

No sign of Sadie. *Good.* She crushed herself against the side of the farthest shed.

Simeon opened the door of the shed attached to the silo. A loud stream of expletives greeted him.

A woman's voice.

Emily.

The door closed. Liz dashed to the silo, edging through its metal door. The tall structure was largely empty, waiting to be restocked after the coming harvest. The remaining heaps of long-fermented silage smelled tobacco-y, irritating her throat and nose. Little light filtered from the top, but she detected Sadie was also inside the silo, crouched near the shed's back door, her ear pressed against it. Liz gestured toward the silage, pulled out a small flashlight, and silently began to search among the piles.

Was Kiera here or in the shed?

Liz didn't want to dig.

She didn't want to uncover . . . anything.

A moan!

Like a bulldozer, she pushed piles of the pungent stuff aside.

Kiera!

Trussed like a lamb for the slaughter, her green eyes glowed with terror.

Liz grabbed for the girl's gag, but the soft snap of fingers whipped Liz around toward Sadie.

"Hide!" Sadie mouthed. She burrowed behind the closest pile of silage. Liz dove behind another on the opposite side of the silo. With sweaty, smelly fingers, she yanked the pepper spray from her shorts pocket and tried to smother her reverberating breaths.

Light spilled into the silo as the shed's door burst open.

"This wasn't the plan." Simeon strode ahead of Emily, who was drawing a small, deadly looking pistol from her bag.

She's still wearing a suit. Though petrified, Liz's brain noted that Emily had changed to more sensible shoes. She was a meticulous planner—of evil.

Simeon turned, standing between the woman and where Kiera lay. "I won't have such violence on my farm."

Emily laughed, a sound more blasphemous than her earlier expletives. "You know I'm all for freedom of religion, Simeon, but it's a little late for you to exercise your tender conscience."

"You should never have come here."

"And leave it to *you* take care of Peabody?"

Liz saw only the back of Emily's neatly arranged dark hair, but she could imagine the curl of the woman's pink lip.

"You would have let him destroy everything," Emily sneered. "Everything I've worked for."

"Everything *you've* worked for?" Simeon shook with rage. "What about my life? My family and community? My reputation? You never told me you meant to kill Clarence. You even tried to implicate *me* with that awl."

Emily's shoulders rose in a shrug. "Not necessarily. But it worked out."

"Worked out?" he thundered, his eyes dangerous. "And now, because you made a stupid mistake—"

"Be quiet, Simeon."

Her tone sent a wild shiver through Liz.

Emily half-raised her pistol. "The girl was weeding—wrong place, wrong time. Heard too much. She's just one of those little surprises that has to be dealt with."

You *have to be dealt with.* Liz gritted her teeth. Though she'd silenced her phone, texting Sadie probably would betray her presence since she was so close to the two criminals. But Sadie was farther away.

A message popped up on Liz's screen. *S,* it read, *10 sec.*

Sadie was gunning for Simeon. In ten seconds.

Liz, pepper spray in hand, poised to spring at Emily. 10—9—8—7—6—

God, help us!

3—2—

Whang! Clunk!

Even as Liz heard the metallic sound of something smacking Simeon, she sprang and sprayed Emily, tackling her in the process. As they fell forward, Liz knocked the gun from the choking woman's hand, only to feel vicious elbows in her ribs that made her drop the pepper spray. It rolled away, its echo bouncing off the cement walls.

Gasping, she grabbed handfuls of Emily's hair.

Grunts of pain sounded. Liz, still lying atop her enemy, yanked harder. *Bald Emily. I'd love that.* Sadie swung her shovel at Simeon again—

Liz's back suddenly slammed onto the cement floor with a sickening crunch. *So . . . much . . . pain. How did she manage to flip me?*

"Liz!" Sadie yelled, still grasping her shovel. She turned on Emily.

The cold barrel of a gun jammed into Liz's temple as Emily snarled, "Stop or I'll shoot her."

"Oh no you won't."

Mary Ann's voice!

Liz opened her eyes. Emily, lips drawn back from bared teeth, glared down at her with such hate that she wanted to close her eyes again.

But she could see Mary Ann standing in the shed's doorway, leveling a long gun at Emily. "Drop it, Emily. Or whoever you are. If you think I don't know how to use this shotgun, just try me. I'd love to turn you into puree."

Though Emily's face still twisted with rage, the pistol fell to the ground.

Mary Ann ordered, "Move away from Liz. Now."

Emily complied. Sadie scooped up the pistol and pointed it at Emily. "Liz, are you okay? Can you call 911?"

"Thank you. Oh, thank you." Liz exhaled for what seemed the first time in an hour. "I'm so glad you came when you did."

Mary Ann didn't take her eyes off Emily as she said, "Could have been here sooner, but I think that detour to fetch my gun was worth it."

"It was." Aching with pain and triumph, Liz slowly sat up and pulled out her phone. But she froze at the sight of Simeon.

He lay inert on the cement floor, sweaty hair pushed back from his lined, farmer-white forehead. Despite blood trickling from wounds Sadie had inflicted, Liz saw something that jarred her anew and made the room spin.

21

"Liz!" her friends chorused. "Are you all right?"

"Lie down," Mary Ann commanded.

"I'm fine." Liz dialed 911. "It's just that I finally found the star."

Sadie and Mary Ann both gave her curious looks. "What star?"

Emily scoffed. "I hit her good, didn't I? No brain left—"

"Shut up." Sadie waved the pistol menacingly.

"I'll tell you about it later." Liz ignored her roiling stomach and turned to her phone. Officer Dixon, sounding stunned, promised to come immediately.

Liz leaped to her feet. Adrenaline probably masked her body's painful hints of injury. "We have to untie Kiera!"

Still pointing her gun at Emily, Mary Ann shrugged off her shoulder bag. "Open it, Liz. I always carry a pocket knife and a pair of sharp scissors."

Sadie found rope in the shed with which to bind Emily and Simeon. Liz hastened to Kiera and yanked out her gag.

The girl could only whimper. Liz threw her arms around her, and then began to saw at the thick ropes chafing the teen's wrists and ankles.

"Thank you. Thank you," Kiera mumbled again and again. As color returned to the girl's face, so did her usual attitude. "That *witch*!"

"We all fell for her lies." Liz cut the last rope and hugged her young employee again. "Don't think about that now. Let's just be thankful nobody else died."

At least, not yet. Liz wasn't sure Emily would survive until the police came. Sadie yanked mercilessly at her arms as she bound her.

Kiera trembled with anger, never taking her cat eyes off Emily.

"You're a liar. A dirty, filthy *liar.* I don't know if I'll ever trust librarians again."

Thankfully, Officer Dixon arrived, heard their preliminary statements, and handcuffed the prisoners, escorting Emily to the patrol car first. Simeon, who had awakened, gave Liz a look she'd never forget.

Then he bowed his head as the officer marched him past his weeping wife, daughters, and grandchildren, and his stony-faced sons and brothers.

"I was right about that woman all along!" Sadie crowed for the umpteenth time, waving her chocolate croissant like a flag.

"You were right!" Liz and the other Material Girls saluted her with their own croissants.

"Back at the silo, I certainly didn't think we'd end up here tonight." Liz cast a grateful eye around the tasteful peace of Naomi's Sweet Everything bakery. "Bless you, everyone." She hugged Mary Ann and Sadie, on either side of her. "You saved my life. You saved Kiera's life, and Isaac's, and who knows how many others."

"You're the one who deserves the hurrahs," Mary Ann said as everyone cheered. "If you hadn't kept plugging away, trying to find out the real murderer's identity, I don't think anyone would have discovered the truth."

A flush of pleasure heated Liz's cheeks. She turned to their hostess. "Thanks, Naomi, for opening up for us so late."

Naomi poured Liz a fresh cup of coffee and hugged her again. "Thank God you're all safe and those people are behind bars."

"I think Kiera's mother is thankful too." Upon arriving at Simeon's farm, the white-faced woman had held her daughter close. Kiera had clung to her as they walked back to her mother's battered sedan.

"Now that it's over, and we're all safe and sound"—Mary Ann leaned forward and pierced Liz with her knowing gaze—"maybe you can tell us what's really been going on?"

"I suppose that might be a good idea," Liz teased. She slowly stirred cream into her coffee. "I'm still not sure about some details with this case. But the chief asked me to meet with him tomorrow morning to review everything. I hope he answers my questions. For example, who was Isaac protecting?"

"Just tell us what you know." Even Opal's calm demeanor had vanished.

"Well, to begin, Sadie and I heard Simeon say Emily killed Clarence Peabody," Liz said, "and she as good as admitted it. Since then, I wondered how she managed to do it, because I saw Emily sunbathing on the pier all afternoon that day. That's what I told Chief Houghton, which probably eliminated her as a suspect in his mind."

Sadie cocked her head. "If anybody could pull it off, that lying hussy could. But how?"

"I thought back to what she wore that day," Liz answered, "a long robe over her bathing suit and a floppy, polka-dotted hat. Before she slipped away to meet Clarence, she must have swathed a pillow dummy with the robe and positioned the hat so it appeared she still lay on the pier, at least from a distance."

"Whoa." Caitlyn's eyes, with their bright blue eyeliner, widened. "She meant to do him in from the beginning."

"Absolutely." Rage boiled in Liz again, but she commanded her emotions to cease and desist. "Emily's real name is Jennifer Clayton. I don't yet know her exact connection with Richard Clayton, who not only helped pull off the Countryside Commons swindle here in Indiana, but possibly one in Kentucky and one in Ohio. But Emily obviously was in the middle of it. Maybe even in charge."

"What kind of swindle?" Opal asked.

Liz described what she'd discovered about the land's asbestos contamination and Midwest Services' disappearance, leaving Clarence Peabody legally obligated to clean up the land.

"He was an awful man," Sadie said, "but he had reason to be upset—losing the land and his company."

"Especially when he realized that Meister Builders and Simeon Graber, who later repurchased the foreclosed land and made a big profit, were reborn versions of Midwest Services and Abe Brenneman, the front man who had talked him into the Countryside Commons deal in the first place.

"Peabody tracked Abe/Simeon to Pleasant Creek. When Emily sensed major trouble, she, as a higher-up in Midwest Services, offered to meet with him to help work things out."

"She worked them out, all right." Naomi shuddered. "What a scary woman."

"Amen to that." Liz still could feel the barrel of that little pistol pressed to her temple. She shook off a shiver. "She'd do anything to protect her profits."

Caitlyn growled, "I can't believe she quilted with us."

"I feel like disinfecting Sew Welcome from top to bottom," Mary Ann said. "But I'll limit it to my scissors and sewing machines." A gleam of curiosity lit her dark eyes. "Back in the silo, you said something about finding a star. You said you'd explain later."

"A star?" the others asked in unison.

Liz exhaled. She'd kept her family quest private all this time. Like her mother, she'd held her secret close. But now seemed like the perfect moment to tell these women, who had become her sisters.

"The star is linked to my mother, Abigail Byler Eckardt, an Amish girl from Pleasant Creek who ran away to Boston," she began. "But I didn't know that until she died and left me her diary."

Her rapt audience listened as Liz continued, "I read a section in which she was dealing with Boston's Christmas season and noted that few seemed to follow Bethlehem's star to worship Jesus. Then she wrote something about a star that didn't shine so pure elsewhere and a man who would do anything for profit."

The other Material Girls looked at each other with raised eyebrows.

"What'd you see in the silo?" Sadie demanded. "I didn't see any star there."

"I saw the star on Simeon's forehead, close to his hairline," Liz answered. "A birthmark, in the perfect shape of a star, usually hidden by his hair or hat."

"Are you saying Simeon had some connection with your mother?" Opal's own forehead furrowed.

"That's what she's saying." Mary Ann turned to Liz. "I'm only 95 percent sure, but I think your mother's real name was Deborah Miller."

"Deborah Miller?" Liz paused. "Deborah . . ." The name finally clicked in Liz's mind. That was one of the runaway Amish girls mentioned in the newspaper articles she'd found in the library!

Mary Ann continued, "I thought I recognized her in your photo, and I mentioned her to you. She was the girl who used to work with me at my mother's sewing shop." The older woman put gentle hands on Liz's shoulders. "At the time Deborah ran away, Simeon Graber was courting her."

"Miss Eckardt, would you please join me at the county jail tomorrow?" Bishop Manz usually exuded strength and authority. Tonight, as he stood at Liz's front door, his bent shoulders and distraught face defined him as a weary old man. "Simeon needs to speak with you."

Still reeling, Liz wanted to slam the door just like he had. She'd reassured herself repeatedly that Simeon was not her father. Her birth had taken place years after her mother's flight to Boston. And Liz's features resembled the father she knew.

Still, she never wanted to see Simeon again. Ever.

"All right," she told the bishop. They agreed to meet at the jail at ten thirty, after Liz spoke with Chief Houghton.

Unable to sleep, Liz attacked her neglected work at the inn. Like Mary Ann, she felt like hosing down every inch of the Rose of Sharon room and the Sunrise room, where Emily had stayed. Liz contented herself with scrubbing and waxing floors until they gleamed.

Finally, she fell into bed, but she dreamed of the barn raising, and in her dream, she served chocolate croissants to Simeon, who was wearing a long Abe Lincoln coat and top hat.

"Let's get this over with," Liz muttered to herself as she dressed the next morning. Though, of course, this would not prove the end of her contact with Simeon. She'd have to testify at his trial.

Liz's day brightened, though, when she arrived at the police station.

Chief Houghton thanked her for her excellent detective work. Then he added, "Though it's a wonder you and your friends weren't killed."

She reviewed with him what they'd briefly discussed the night before: her take on Simeon's and Emily's roles in the fraudulent deals, Peabody's killing, and Kiera's kidnapping.

Now Liz had time to tell him about her research on Richard Clayton. "His name is on the paperwork for the Countryside Commons deal," she said, "and evidently for the land sales in Zanesville, Ohio, and Paducah, Kentucky, as well. But I'd only begun to check him out."

"So far, Jennifer Clayton isn't talking," the chief said, frowning. "But we'll find him. We already found the guy who harassed you on the interstate. A small-time troublemaker Simeon hired to frighten you."

"He succeeded." *So Simeon's talking?* "Did Simeon write that note too?"

The chief nodded. "Yes, but according to him, Jennifer came up with the idea and also slipped it into your mailbox."

Yes, Emily—Jennifer—had arrived that very day. She'd also been in the area when Liz's quilt had been slashed.

"He said Emily vandalized your quilt too." Chief Houghton seemed to have read her mind, though he shook his head sheepishly. "I should have realized that was a woman's crime, committed by someone who understood its personal value."

Liz didn't want to alienate the chief, but she had to know. "I'm puzzled about a couple of things. Early on, I suspected Jeremiah Yoder of killing Peabody because Peabody had harassed Sarah."

"I thought of that too. But he was training horses with his family at the time of the murder. A dozen witnesses saw him."

That answers that. But Liz needed to know more. "Initially, I'm sure you considered us all suspects. You weeded us out, but how did Emily slip through?"

The chief's face reddened. "After interviewing her, I called the library where she supposedly worked. They confirmed Emily Hart's employment there but said she was on vacation, which matched what she'd told me. Given that you saw her sunbathing on the pier during the time of Peabody's murder—"

"She fooled me there," Liz admitted, and told him her suspicions about the dummy "Emily" dressed in her beachwear.

"Then all the physical evidence pointed to Isaac," the chief said, "so I had no reason to further investigate her until Officer Dixon called me at the conference and told me about Kiera's disappearance." He grimaced. "Dixon had run the photo you gave him through the Bureau of Motor Vehicles and found it matched an Indiana license under the name of Jennifer Clayton, not an Ohio one belonging to Emily Hart. I'd already decided to leave the training early, and then Dixon called while on his way to Simeon's farm." Houghton shook his head. "That woman is a piece of work. Digging a little deeper, I found that the real Emily Hart who works at the Columbus, Ohio, library is Jennifer Clayton's cousin. Jennifer knew Emily was going on vacation and assumed her identity when she came to Pleasant Creek."

She thought she had her bases covered. But the killer didn't factor in qualities like small-town friendship, loyalty, and justice for the innocent and the guilty alike.

Liz grinned. Emily also couldn't have begun to imagine someone like Sadie the Crazy Quilter who, cut from a different cloth, zeroed in on lies and deception.

Other questions swam inside Liz, but she had to know the answer to the most important one: "Has Isaac been freed yet?"

"Not quite yet." At her impatient gesture, he nodded. "I know. We should just let him walk out of here. We will, once Jennifer Clayton and Simeon are brought up on charges and the paperwork is completed—you can be sure of that."

Okay, one more question. "Do you know why he let everyone think he killed Peabody?"

"He told the bishop and me last night when we informed him of Emily's and Simeon's arrests." Chief Houghton's eyes softened. "He was protecting Sarah."

"Sarah? But she was at home at the time of the murder. She was never under suspicion," Liz protested, "unless, like Kiera, she'd seen or heard something incriminating—"

"Sarah didn't witness the murder. Isaac did. Emily wore gloves, of course, when she stabbed Clarence. She forced Isaac at gunpoint to hold the murder weapon and dump the body into the lake." Houghton swore under his breath. "Fingerprints, DNA, bloodstains—she lined up a great case against Isaac. She'd also seen Sarah and him together earlier and figured that threatening to kill his girlfriend would keep him quiet. She was right."

Another "little surprise" Emily had dealt with. Liz shuddered. To think, she herself had felt safer after the quilt slashing with Emily under her roof! If Naomi hadn't stayed that night . . .

Thankfully, a rap on the chief's door interrupted Liz's imaginings. The female officer informed them Bishop Manz had arrived. As she stood, Chief Houghton thanked her again and told her he'd keep her posted as new information was discovered about the cases.

Liz steeled herself as she and the bishop endured the usual questions and searches. Walking into the visitation area with him, Liz breathed a prayer, sat, and looked into Simeon's "honest" face.

22

If Isaac appeared odd in an orange prison jumpsuit, Simeon looks positively alien.

Liz made no effort to break the silence.

At last, Simeon said, "I suppose you know I was involved in the Countryside Commons project?"

Liz enunciated each word with care. "You mean, your fraud that bilked Clarence Peabody out of his business?"

The man's bearded chin fell, but he said, "Ja. That is what I mean."

"I don't know all the ins and outs." Liz crossed her arms. "But I think I get the picture. You helped Richard and Jennifer Clayton victimize small businesses in order to build their little empire."

"Not little." Simeon shook his head. "A large one throughout the Midwest. But Richard isn't part of it."

"What do you mean, he's not involved?" Liz hissed. "You signed as his representative for the purchase of Countryside Commons."

"True." Simeon spoke slowly, as if every breath cost him great effort. "But Richard, Jennifer's father, has been in a Chicago nursing home for years. He has no idea what he signs. Or what Jennifer's representatives sign in his name."

What depths of evil could one woman reach? But if he thought Jennifer's sins would distract Liz from his, Simeon had another thing coming. "So Countryside Commons was only one 'project.' But it ultimately resulted in Clarence's murder."

He winced as if she had struck him. "You overheard me back at the silo. I wanted no part of violence."

"Yet you contributed to it by cooperating with it."

"Ja." His hoarse voice broke. "I did. Countryside Commons wasn't my only project. Like mein Vater before me, I have, every decade or so, helped work out a similar construction agreement."

Liz stared at Simeon and then at Bishop Manz's drawn, immovable face. Not only Manz's nephew, but his sister's husband had practiced long-term deception.

"Why, Simeon?" The bishop's lips barely moved.

"Vater wanted more for me than he could provide." Simeon dropped his head. "I wanted more."

For your children and grandchildren? Or for a different life?

"You and your father must have worked very hard to preserve your reputations," Liz said, sarcasm lacing her words.

He flinched. "Ja. But somehow, Deborah found out."

All the oxygen drained from the room. Liz choked out, "You mean Deborah Miller? My mother?"

"Ja." Now he could not meet her gaze at all. "We were planning to marry that fall. We were about to be published. But she found out. She told me she could not marry a liar and a thief. She said she would tell the bishop and elders the truth."

Liz leaped to her feet, burning as if he'd aimed a torch at her. "Did you threaten to kill her? Is that why she ran away?"

"No. No. I could never kill Deborah. Never." His eyes moistened. "But . . . I did threaten her family if she told—"

"Just like Emily threatened to kill Sarah." Liz clenched her hands, longing to claw the man's face, to etch pain deep into him, the way he'd hurt her mother.

"I didn't mean it. I wouldn't have done it." Simeon covered his face with a calloused hand. "But she thought I would. And I lost her."

Liz bared her teeth. "You deserved to lose her."

He whispered, "I know."

The vacuum that followed flattened Liz's lungs. How had Simeon lived years—no, decades—crazed with such wicked greed?

Finally, the older man wiped his damp face and beard with a

spotless handkerchief. "If only I could ask her pardon."

"You're too late," Liz skewered him. "She died six months ago."

At the despair in his eyes, her anger lessened a fraction.

"When you bought the inn," Simeon said, "I heard someone mention that your mother had passed away. And when I saw you at the barn raising, I knew you were Deborah's daughter. Other than your coloring, you don't resemble her. I assume you look like your father. But your voice, your expressions, the way you hold your head . . . I knew." A tiny, wry smile touched his lips. "And like Deborah, you tolerate nothing but the truth."

Simeon did know Mom. She wanted to deny it, but couldn't.

"I cannot ask her pardon." He riveted desperate eyes to Liz's. "But I ask for yours."

Her jaw came unhinged. *Forgive* him? The man who had terrorized her mother, had broken her heart, had aided in a hundred ugly acts, all while wearing a super-righteous guise? She wished Sadie's shovel was handy.

On second thought, she was thankful it wasn't. The orange jumpsuit would look lousy on her too.

Memories of her mother's warm presence, almost as tangible as her quilt, wrapped around Liz's rigid shoulders. Her mom's voice whispered: *I forgave him.*

She had, Liz realized with a start. Her mother *had* left anger and pain behind to grow a new, productive life. She had not allowed bitterness to cling to her like a parasite, sucking away her joy in living.

Bishop Manz waited, expressionless. Were his calm eyes scanning her soul?

Simeon waited, his face bleak as his future.

Liz extended her hand. "I forgive you, Simeon."

Cars and buggies crowded the Olde Mansion Inn's parking. Liz, standing at the front door, greeted a stream of smiling English and Amish guests who had come to join in the celebration. She tried not to remember a similar onslaught when the news of Clarence Peabody's murder had broken.

Thankfully, Liz's open house today commemorated joyful events: Kiera's survival, Isaac's freedom, the inn's grand opening, and the kickoff for the schoolchildren's clothing drive—with the Material Girls out in full force.

For several days, they had helped Liz ready the inn for the Pleasant Creek party of the decade.

"Second to the shivaree, of course." Mary Ann grinned wickedly. As usual, she had things well in hand. This time, Liz had cheered her on.

Mary Ann had not only baked innumerable pies, but also invited her county-fair competitors, including Sadie and Opal, to outdo themselves. Naomi had brought trays of fragrant sweet rolls. Caitlyn had baked butter cakes that she and the others had stayed up half the previous night to assemble into a frosted replica of the Olde Mansion Inn.

"That is spectacular." Jackson Cross, spectacular himself in khakis and a white golf shirt, stopped in front of the cake table, licking his lips.

"First, let me take a picture!" Liz aimed her camera at the cake. It featured barn-red frosting, white-sugared gingerbread "woodwork," and all the turrets and gables that made the Olde Mansion Inn so lovely. Kiera's flower beds had been duplicated with fondant, jelly beans, and hard candies.

Jackson shook his head. "I could eat the whole first floor myself, but are you really going to cut that gorgeous thing?"

"You bet. Cakes are for eating." Sadie, standing behind the table, brandished a large knife. "Do you want the front porch or the back?"

"Front." He also helped himself to peach pie. "Carrot sticks? Broccoli? Who eats that stuff when all this incredible food is just waiting for a fork?"

Liz grinned. "I had to try to offset all the sugar."

"I'll take one of each, just to make you feel better." His teasing smile morphed into open admiration. "Say, I hear you not only throw a great party, but have been made an honorary detective on the police force."

"Oh, nothing like that." Her cheeks warmed. "I just wanted to help Isaac and his family."

He lowered his voice. "I couldn't believe he murdered Peabody either. If you hadn't come to Pleasant Creek, though, he might have been jailed for life. Instead"—Jackson's grin returned—"that kid just helped himself to three pieces of pie."

Liz followed Jackson's gesture. Sure enough, Isaac had loaded his plate. However, he seemed to have forgotten all about it, mesmerized by Sarah serving coffee at the beverage table, her face under her Kapp rosy and happy again. Several shared smiles crossed between them like telepathic kisses. Miriam, behind her son, touched his arm, and he followed her across the room to greet Liz.

"I think someone wants to talk to you." Jackson excused himself, inserting a check into the nearby Clothe Our Kids donation box.

"I-I can't tell you how much I appreciate all the risks you've taken for me." Balancing his plate in one palm, Isaac grasped Liz's hand. "I can't thank you enough."

"My pleasure," Liz said. "Of course, I expect a lot from you today, Isaac." Confusion crisscrossed his face until she pointed at the inn-cake. "You have to help us make that disappear!"

"I'll do my best, Miss Eckardt!" He charged across the room to commandeer another plate.

Miriam's indigo eyes shone like a sunlit sky. For a moment, she and Liz simply steeped in each other's joy. Miriam murmured, "I knew Isaac was in Gött's hands. I am so thankful He sent you to help rescue him."

Liz laughed ruefully. "Mary Ann had to rescue me. I couldn't have done anything without the Material Girls."

"What would we all do if we could not count on each other?" Miriam squeezed her hand.

Liz would have loved to spend more time with her, but hostess duties called. Still, she couldn't recall when she'd enjoyed her obligations more. She knew so many people now—downtown businessmen, her pastor and fellow church members, girls she'd worked with at the barn raising, children and parents from Beans's birthday party, new friends she'd made at quilting classes. The Louisville quilters even came too.

"When we heard what happened, I nearly swallowed my teeth," Vera drawled. "To think that sweet little Emily's a murderer!"

"I can't believe she tried to drag me into it," Jill fumed. "I guess she said I was joining her here so she'd look even more innocent while she did her dirty work."

"We're just glad it's over." Liz repeated that line, along with thanks for compliments about her bravery, a hundred times. When the drill began to wear on her, she sent up little prayers of thanksgiving. The outcome could have been so different.

Gene Peabody surprised her by accepting her invitation. "You're one pushy woman, you know that?" The way he pumped her hand up and down told her she'd earned his respect, even if she was a lawyer.

She noticed Chief Houghton, surrounded by townspeople, patiently answering questions while his coffee cooled and cake went untasted. Liz moved to his side, answered a few herself, and gradually edged him away as Mary Ann and Sadie took over with a hilarious version of the rescue that might live on for generations as a rural legend.

"Had enough interrogations?" She replaced the chief's tepid cup with a steaming one.

He chuckled. "I'm used to it. Folks just want to know what's going on."

"I think you deserve to eat one piece of cake minus questions."

"I'll drink to that." He sipped his coffee with pleasure. "I really have appreciated your help with this case, Liz."

"And I appreciate that you didn't write me off as a crazy lawyer lady." He hadn't swallowed all her theories, but he'd listened.

"I wish all the crazies I deal with were like you." He shook his head. "Speaking of crazies, we've found more businesses Jennifer Clayton had conned. Her dad, Richard, once ran a legitimate company in Chicago, but when he went downhill, she seized control and used its assets to pull off her heists. Remember that phone call to Chicago Kiera heard? Jennifer was talking to her main money man there." He grimaced. "Smart, smart woman. Scary."

"You're telling me."

"But you outsmarted her." He grinned. "Some people want me to deputize you. Insist on it, in fact."

"No thanks. I have enough to do here." She waved as she resumed her place at the front door to greet the late arrivals.

She paused to kneel and scratch Beans's ears. Despite exhaustion from all the excitement, he condescended to open one eye and emit a small moan of ecstasy.

"He did lots better with his bath this time." Kiera knelt to take over for Liz. "I don't know what got into him that day he ran off and shook all over that poor hippie lady."

"At that point, we all were a little messed up, Beans included." Liz threw her arms around the girl. "How are you doing? Are the nightmares still bothering you?"

"Not quite as much." Her lip crinkled. "Last night, in my dreams, I shot Emily with a water gun. Right in the face."

"Awesome! I hope I have that dream tonight." After several weeks, Liz's own nightmares hadn't graduated to such harmlessness, but she was beginning to sleep more and lie awake less.

Kiera snapped her fingers. "Oh, I wanted to let you know. If it's okay with you, Sarah asked me to take her place serving coffee for an hour this afternoon."

"Sarah asked?" Liz stared. "And you're doing it?"

"She said she was sorry she jumped all over my case." Kiera shrugged. "I think we're both tired of being mad."

Liz agreed, of course, but she was puzzled. After all the drama, an anticlimactic end to World War III? She'd take it, though. She'd certainly take it.

Liz looked up to see Kiera's mother, Stacy, enter. She stood and extended her hand. "I'm so glad you came today."

Stacy nodded. "Wanted to drop in and thank you." A stale-cigarette aura surrounded the heavyset woman clad in tight, faded jeans. She shifted from foot to foot.

"I'm sorry such a terrible thing happened to Kiera, Stacy." *If only I'd caught onto Emily's act earlier.*

"Sure wasn't your fault. Wasn't Kiera's neither." She went on to express loudly how glad she was the police had put those rotten so-and-sos behind bars. Her daughter tucked her head and continued petting Beans.

"I coulda lost my girl." Stacy's hard face suddenly melted. "I coulda lost my baby." She touched Kiera's head.

The teen looked up, and though she rolled her eyes, a wave of hunger crossed her face.

Stroking Kiera's head awkwardly, Stacy said to Liz, "I just wanted you to know that I'm gonna try and do better by her."

"Good." Liz directed Stacy to the food, thanked her again for coming, and left the two to what she hoped was a positive conversation.

The rest of the afternoon blended into a fun mix of chitchat and celebration. Near the open house's end, Sadie quieted the still large crowd with a piercing whistle, and Mary Ann announced the result of the Clothe Our Kids drive. "Today, because of the generosity of the people and businesses of Pleasant Creek, we have raised more than two thousand dollars!"

Cheers resounded as the high school and elementary principals accepted the check.

Kiera and other kids like her will wear warm clothes this winter. Liz, gathering dirty dishes, paused to let her own warm feeling sink in.

Wait. Was Mary Ann calling her to the front of the room?

"Liz Eckardt, I mean *you*!" Her friend waved an imperious hand.

Okay. Liz set down the tray and joined the other Material Girls at Mary Ann's side.

"I'm sure we all want to express our appreciation for Liz's opening the Olde Mansion Inn for our town party this afternoon."

It was officially Liz's open house, not Pleasant Creek's, but she didn't mind. Mary Ann waited for the applause to die down and then continued, "Liz came here, expecting peace and quiet. Instead, we all were shocked by a terrible murder. But Liz did not leave. She not only invested in this beautiful inn, she invested in our community. At great risk to herself, she helped bring wrongdoers to justice.

"We hope this little gift will express how glad we are that you came to Pleasant Creek." Mary Ann handed Liz a beautifully wrapped, black-and-white package.

"Th-thank you," Liz stuttered. "Believe me, I wouldn't be standing here today without my friends' help." Amid more cheers, she opened the gift.

Her mom's quilt. It was mended and looked as if no wicked hand had ever defaced it.

The rest of the open house blurred into a mass of smiles, thanks, hugs, and goodbyes. But one person stood out.

Miriam.

Wearing a strangely radiant smile, she examined the quilt. "What lovely, lovely work." Then she invited Liz to her house the following afternoon.

Liz stared. "Are you sure?"

Miriam nodded as her husband joined her.

Liz blinked. How could she have missed Philip's presence?

His expression changed little, but he said, "Please come."

Later, as Liz cuddled with her quilt, no nightmares marred her sleep. But questions, like restless lambs, wandered through her head all night long.

23

Fighting Sunday afternoon drowsiness as she pulled into Miriam's driveway, Liz waved at her friend who stood on the porch.

"Please come inside." Miriam steered her into the house as soon as Liz mounted the front steps. "Everyone's busy elsewhere, so we have it to ourselves."

How like Miriam. The living room was simple. No cushions on the chairs, of course, or brightly colored pillows, pictures, or other decor. It would have been plain except for the highly polished wooden floors, the quiet artistry of neutral-color rag rugs, and the unique arrangements of handcrafted furniture. A crock of multicolored roses, their beauty enhanced by understated surroundings, glowed on a small table.

But they held Liz's attention for a moment only.

A baby quilt, spread on a larger table, magnetized her gaze. Her mouth went dry. "My mother's quilt."

"No." Shaking her head, Miriam wore the same luminous smile as she had at the open house. "*My* mother's quilt."

Liz grasped the edge of the table to steady herself. "What was your mother's name?"

"Martha Hilty Fischer." Miriam pointed to the initials E.H. on her quilt. "Her grandmother Esther Hilty made identical quilts for her granddaughters born close together—my mother, Martha, and"—she clasped Liz's hands—"your mother, Deborah Miller Eckardt."

"So we're second cousins?" Part of Liz danced for joy; part of her longed for a closer bond.

"Officially, I suppose." Miriam hugged her. "In our hearts, I believe we are sisters."

They returned to the porch to enjoy the breeze. The corn wasn't yet tall enough to shut it out. They drank lemonade and shared stories of growing up in different worlds. Liz told her about the jolt she experienced on receiving her mother's diary. "I wish she'd told me sooner about her upbringing. About her family. Even if it meant having to expose Simeon Graber."

"Thanks be to Gött she left you that diary," Miriam said, "or you might never have found your way back to Pleasant Creek."

"Is that a buggy?" Liz peered down the gravel road at a dust cloud in the distance.

"Two, I believe." Miriam stood, her dress flapping in the wind. "My family's returning. They'll be ready for lemonade. Would you like to help me?"

The rumble of buggy wheels drew nearer as Liz filled glasses with ice from an old-fashioned icebox while Miriam poured.

For the first time that afternoon, uncertainty wobbled into the room. Liz still wondered how well Philip would tolerate her. If extended family came, they might not take kindly to her company, especially inside the house. "Will my presence here upset anyone? Perhaps I should leave."

"Not unless you want to."

The disappointment in her face reassured Liz. "All right, I'll stay awhile." As she helped finish preparations, the small spot of exultation inside her grew. Miriam considered her family. That was enough.

Together they walked to the front porch as the buggies rolled into the driveway. Isaac pulled the first buggy to a stop. His face lit up as he greeted Liz. Grace and Keturah jumped out, and then Isaac and his three younger brothers took the buggy to the barn. Keturah danced around Liz with the uninhibited joy expressed best by six-year-olds. Grace, too, seemed glad to see Liz. If Philip indeed became more accepting, she would see the twelve-year-old more often and savor the likeness to her mom.

When Philip stepped from the second buggy and approached

them, Liz's muscles tensed. But he removed his Sunday hat and smiled. "Welcome. I am glad you could come today."

He still sounded stiff, but his smile warmed the planes of his face. Liz smiled back. "I wouldn't have missed it for the world."

An older couple had exited the buggy, and Miriam led Liz down the steps to greet them. The man was tall and lanky, with sandy, graying hair. His unblinking eyes focused on her. Liz was sure she'd never met him, yet he seemed familiar.

But when her gaze shifted to the woman, Liz's stomach lurched. She couldn't tell if their visitor was younger or older than her mother had been. But those blue-gray eyes, the shape of her face, her sideways smile that trembled at the sight of Liz—

"Liz, this is your mother's younger sister, Ruth Miller Hammel." Miriam's quiet tone belied the fireworks in her face. "And this is Amos Miller, your mother's older brother."

She'd sacrificed her old life for this moment. A thousand words tangled in her throat. "H-hello."

Hello? That's all she could say?

Her aunt Ruth, however, said it all. "I was so sure my big sister would come home someday," she sobbed as she enfolded Liz in chubby arms. "I prayed every night. Gött forgive me, I thought He had not heard my prayer.

"He did not answer as I thought He should. But Gött *has* answered." She ran work-worn hands over Liz's wet cheeks. "And I am thankful I have lived to see this day."

EPILOGUE

A few months later . . .

Liz had never sat through a three-hour church service and certainly not one that was spoken entirely in Swiss. But as she shifted quietly to awaken muscles paralyzed by the hard bench, she affirmed to herself that it was worth it.

She sat beside Aunt Ruth and her cousins Phoebe and Tabitha on the women's side of the Yoders' barn. Sarah's and Isaac's earnest young faces shone as they stood before the elders, answering their questions. The young couple had endured church discipline for their lies and unauthorized rendezvous, but, in light of all they had suffered, their sins had been forgiven. Miriam, seated with her girls and sisters near the front, radiated such joy Liz could almost forget that a few months ago, her son had languished in jail.

After the bishop's blessing and prayers by the couple's fathers, the service finally ended. Almost as one, the women scurried to the house to finish wedding feast preparations while men set up tables and moved benches.

As Liz walked to the kitchen with the others, she drank in the brisk autumn air, the fragrant rustling of the last corn shocks. Bright pumpkins dotted the fields, and rich clumps of jewel-color chrysanthemums crowded the Yoders' flower beds.

The other Material Girls, armed with aprons and side dishes, waved at Liz as they walked from the parking field.

"I'm so glad the weather cooperated today. They can feed some of this crowd outside," Mary Ann said.

"There must be several hundred people here," Liz marveled.

Her friends had been invited to share the wedding feast, but not the service. Once again, Liz realized how strongly family ties bound her to the Amish community.

At the barn raising, she'd been a stranger, clinging to Mary Ann like a shy child. Here, she worked alongside the Material Girls, but she also chatted and laughed with Phoebe and Tabitha as together they sliced innumerable breads, pies, and cakes. Uncle Amos's daughters, Rachel, Dinah, and Hope, smiled and greeted her as they set tables and carried food to the first shift of diners. She didn't know those cousins as well as Aunt Ruth's family, because Uncle Amos, naturally more reserved, had not grafted her into his family's life as Ruth had.

Her aunt was lifting an enormous dish of scalloped potatoes from the oven. Liz grabbed pot holders. "Let me take that."

"You're a good girl, Liz." Ruth allowed her to lug it to the serving table and then gave her a resounding kiss on the cheek. Aunt Ruth wasn't Mom, but she certainly was the next best thing.

Simeon's family did not attend. They were to be shunned seven more months because some of them had suspected his illegal activities but said nothing. Liz pitied them and hoped the Amish community eventually would warm to them again.

When the women ate, she felt comfortable, having learned a little Swiss and a lot more about quilts and Amish cooking. The yodeling still made her crazy, but everyone's relatives had their quirks. She could handle this one—for a few hours.

She stole a little time with Miriam. "Isaac looks so happy. So handsome!"

For once, Miriam did not guard against vanity. "He is wonderful, mein Sön."

After dinner, the bride and groom sought out Liz. Sarah, fresh and lovely in her simple lavender dress, clasped Liz in an unusually demonstrative embrace. "This day would never have come without your help."

"Thank you, cousin," was all Isaac said, but it was enough.

The sweet picture they made and other scenes from the wedding day bonded in Liz's mind like a patchwork quilt: the smiles on usually solemn faces as adults folded strangely idle hands, chatted, and sang; the understated flirting of young men and women in Sunday hats and Kapps; the swarm of small children, giggling, chasing, playing games.

Before she left, Uncle Amos and his sons, Peter, David, Gideon, and little Jesse, greeted her and offered to help with any repairs on her inn.

He was treating her like family. Liz could barely refrain from hugging Amos, but she managed to thank him with appropriate discretion.

Liz returned to the Olde Mansion, glad to trade her dress for jeans. Tomorrow—without Sarah's help—she would finish preparations for a host of weekend guests. How Liz would miss her! But eventually, Sarah would return to work at the inn part-time.

This evening, Liz fetched her mother's quilt from its rack. The gathering darkness outside precluded reading the diary in her favorite spot on the bench. Nevertheless, she removed it from her desk and wandered out to the bench, where she communed with the harvest moon hovering above the shining lake.

Sliding to the side to make room for her mom, she wrapped the quilt around her shoulders and held the diary against her cheek.

And she thanked God and her mother for bringing her home.